# Death By Mistake

## A Josiah Reynolds Mystery
## Book Twenty-Two

# Abigail Keam

**Worker Bee Press**

Published in the USA by

Worker Bee Press
P.O. Box 485
Nicholasville, KY 40340

# Books By Abigail Keam

## The Josiah Reynolds Mysteries
Death By A HoneyBee I
Death By Drowning II
Death By Bridle III
Death By Bourbon IV
Death By Lotto V
Death By Chocolate VI
Death By Haunting VII
Death By Derby VIII
Death By Design IX
Death By Malice X
Death By Drama XI
Death By Stalking XII
Death By Deceit XIII
Death By Magic XIV
Death By Shock XV
Death By Chance XVI
Death By Poison XVII
Death By Greed XVIII
Death By Theft XIX
Death By Betrayal XX
Death By Trauma XXI
Death By Mistake XXII
Death By Mail XXIII

# 1

Hunter Wickliffe woke up. Something had sounded in the night and awakened him. Getting out of bed, he went over to the large double-hung sash window, catching sight of a car racing away around the curve of the driveway to Wickliffe Manor. He could hear the car screech to a stop and then turn onto Old Frankfort Pike. He looked at his watch. It was two twenty-three in the morning.

Donning trousers and flip-flops, Hunter trudged down the hallway and opened the door to his wife's son, Palley's bedroom. The bed was messy, but no Palley. He then slogged to Kathy's room, gently knocked, and opened the bedroom door.

The bed was made, showing no one had slept in it. Odd. His wife usually went to bed around midnight.

After checking the upstairs bathrooms and finding them unoccupied, Hunter went down the grand staircase and searched throughout the entire first floor of his 19th-century home. He couldn't find either

Kathy or Palley.

Hunter checked the decorative ceramic bowl by the open back door and saw Kathy's keys were there. Stepping into the velvet night, he shouted Kathy's name.

No one returned his call.

Thinking it strange Kathy was not in the house, Hunter went outside to look for her. Discovering Kathy's Lexus parked in the driveway, he placed his hand on the hood. Hunter found it cold to the touch, so she had to be on the grounds somewhere. He headed to the stables as he heard the boarded horses acting up. That was always a bad sign.

As he walked down the dark gravel path to the horse barn, a Great Horned Owl hooted in the distance, Black Angus cattle snorted in their pasture, and the crunch-crunch of his flip-flops on the gravel were the only sounds to be heard. The otherwise eerie quiet unnerved Hunter. He made a mental note to get some dogs. Dogs were good indicators of people and things not being in place. They were always aware of the unusual. A dog walking beside him in the dark would give him confidence.

Was he frightened?

Hunter was certainly wary.

Something was definitely off.

He picked up a thick fallen branch from a walnut tree and carried it with him. Closer to the barn, he distinctly heard the horses kicking their stalls and neighing occasionally. Not a good sign. Perhaps a coyote had been sniffing around the stable.

Dropping the branch, Hunter stepped through the side door. Searching for the light switch, he found it and turned on the overhead barn lights. The horses immediately quieted down. He first noticed the pedestal fans, which were supposed to circulate the air on warm nights, were turned off. He looked at his watch again. It was two forty-five. As the night cooled, the fans were programmed to switch off at three.

He stepped to the nearest fan and touched the housing. The metal felt wet. Now what would cause water on the fans? Hunter looked up. The roof wasn't leaking. Besides, it hadn't rained.

"What's going on, ladies?" Hunter asked as he opened the stall doors and checked several horses close to the west entrance until he noticed bales of hay lying in disarray on the floor of the barn's central aisle. Someone or something had also overturned the sweet feed buckets near the storage closet. A sense of dread filled him.

"Kathy? Kathy, are you here?" Hunter called out.

The only responses were horses nickering. Hunter strained to hear his wife's response or maybe a faint cry for help. Perhaps she went to check on the horses and fell. He wanted to hear something—anything resembling a human voice.

Certain that something was amiss, Hunter went into the first five stalls and opened the back stall doors to a large paddock, letting the pregnant Thoroughbred mares out. He brought them in only at night to keep coyotes and wandering dogs away from them. Free, the horses ambled over to a water trough for a quick sip of cool water.

The last four stalls contained pleasure horses boarded at the Wickliffe Farm. Hunter slid open the stall door and grabbed the skittish Arabian horse by the halter. "Whoa, girl. Whoa. That's a good girl." He opened the back exterior door of the stall and pulled the horse toward the outside. She happily joined the other horses now grazing hay left out for them.

Hunter went to the next stall to check on a Quarter horse when he noticed shiny splotches of a dark substance on the center aisle's rubber mat. He squatted down and swiped the dark substance with his finger. The substance was gooey, and as he raised his hand to inspect it, the overhead light illuminated the unmistakable red color. Hunter smelled the red substance and rubbed it between his fingers. As a forensic psychiatrist, he had seen enough dead bodies to know this was coagulated blood!

He jumped up and frantically searched the last stalls. "Kathy! Kathy!" There were two remaining horses, which he quickly pulled into the paddock. It wasn't until Hunter came to the remaining stall that he discovered Kathy lying on her back with unblinking eyes staring at the ceiling. He quickly checked for a pulse, and when he didn't discover one, Hunter slid down the wall of the stall in disbelief. Shocked, he sat beside his dead wife and put his head between his hands, moaned, "Oh, Kathy. What did you do? What did you do?"

# 2

I was working in my beeyard when Charles sped up in a jeep and skidded to a stop on the grass. He waited patiently until I closed a hive and ambled over. Unzipping my hood, I climbed into the jeep, and my English Mastiff, Baby, jumped in the back. Baby had honeybees on his back combing yellow and red pollen into their leg sacks, which I waved away.

"What's up?" I asked, feeling uneasy about his sudden appearance in the bee yard. Was my neighbor and Charles' employer, Lady Elsmere, ill? After all, she was getting up there in years.

"Lady Elsmere has instructed me to fetch you."

"Why, Charles? Is there something wrong?" My heart raced, as I disliked feeling anxiety where my great friend was concerned.

"I'll let Lady Elsmere explain."

I could tell by Charles' nut-brown face he was concerned. Grabbing Charles' hand with my thick beekeeper's glove, I begged, "Please, Charles. Don't keep me in suspense."

"Nothing is wrong with Lady Elsmere. I'll let her explain."

"I can tell by your expression it's bad news. Is it Asa? Has something happened to my daughter?"

"Heavens no. Please calm down, Josiah. Your imagination is running off with you." Charles started for the Big House, which is how the locals referred to Lady Elsmere's mansion.

Since Charles wouldn't say why I was being summoned by Her Ladyship, I sat with arms crossed, but it felt strange. The summons made me fearful. My anxiety was at an all-time high lately, and the smallest thing out of place had me climbing the wall. I guess you could say my overreaction was because of stress. My boyfriend had left me, and my vet had tried to kill me in the past year.

Perhaps Her Ladyship wanting to see me was something as simple as my peacocks making a mess on the hood of her Bentley again. Lady Elsmere didn't like the scratches they left and complained about my birds all the time, but Charles' stoic demeanor was puzzling. No friendly greeting. No teasing. Just stone-faced and silent. Not like Charles at all.

"Charles, stop the jeep! STOP IT NOW!"

Charles slammed on the brakes. "What is it? What's wrong?"

"You either tell me what's going on or I'm getting

out. You're acting weird."

Lady Elsmere's butler took a deep breath and uttered, "Detective Drake is at Lady Elsmere's. He wants to talk to you about Hunter."

"Hunter? Drake is at the Big House about Hunter?"

"Detective Drake didn't know the code to your gate and couldn't reach you by phone, so I was sent to gather you."

"I've turned all the ringers off. I needed a break." Staring at Charles, I waited for him to respond.

Finally, he replied, "Kathy Wickliffe is dead."

The news surprised me, but I didn't see what it had to do with me. The last time I saw Kathy, she was as perky as ever and seemed in perfect health. "Why does Drake want to talk with me? I haven't seen Hunter and Kathy for months."

I was so confused it hadn't hit me what Charles was trying to convey.

"Jo, Hunter has been arrested for Kathy's death. SHE WAS MURDERED!"

# 3

Let me clarify some things first before we go much further.

My name is Josiah Reynolds. I am in my mid-fifties, have red hair, green eyes, walk with a slight limp and wear a hearing aid. I have these infirmities because of a fall off a hundred-foot cliff. It wasn't an accident. A man, who was trying to kill me, pulled me off the cliff. The less said about the attempted murder the better; however, it still gives me the heebie-jeebies to think about it. I should have died, but I bounced off every tree branch going down and finally rested on a ledge forty feet from the top. It took hours and a lot of manpower to lift me off that ledge. I was close to death, but the doctors stabilized me until my daughter, Asa, whisked me away to Key West. Then it was a year of recovery.

That was the first man trying to kill me. There have been others. So, you can understand why I don't like death or being near it.

Well, guess what? Since my fall, I've been a beacon for every murdered corpse in a fifty-mile radius. I have a knack for stumbling over dead bodies. I also have a knack for solving their deaths. It turns out I have a nose for sniffing out the culprits, but I didn't see Kathy Wickliffe's death coming.

The reason I was sitting in Lady Elsmere's stunning walnut-paneled library was Kathy's husband, Hunter, used to be my partner in both solving crime and the bedroom. You get my drift. If you had told me last year that Hunter Wickliffe would have dumped me for his high school flame, I would have called you a liar. Yet, here I was in my stained shorts and sweat-soaked shirt, sitting silent and pale before my nemesis, Detective Drake.

Why is Detective Drake my nemesis, you may ask? I'm really more of a nemesis to him, or at least a thorn in his side. The good detective has shown up at many a crime scene only to find his less-than-favorite beekeeper already there. My frequent success in solving murders annoys him.

I guess I looked a mess, as I was still wearing my bee suit with my hair matted against my skull. Unzipping it, I stepped out of it before folding it up into a nice round ball. I was much cooler sitting in shorts and a T-shirt.

No one said a word as Bess brought in a tray of finger food, a pitcher of iced tea, and bottles of cold water. Bess was Lady Elsmere's chef and Charles's daughter in case you didn't remember. The word *cook* doesn't describe Bess' cooking by a long shot, but I digress.

Lady Elsmere spoke first. "Josiah, would you like a brandy?"

"Yes, please, and can you pour me a glass of tea as well?"

Detective Drake reached over and poured a tall glass of iced tea, handing it to me. For once, he looked sympathetic.

"Thank you. I'm parched." I quickly drained the entire glass.

"Eat some sandwiches. Both of you. Let's make this a civilized grilling," Lady Elsmere quipped.

Drake held up the palm of his hand. "No, thank you." He turned toward me. "I'm here because Kathy Wickliffe was murdered, and I need to ask you some questions."

"Murdered? You sure it was not an accident?" I asked.

"We're quite sure."

"Do you have any suspects? Was Hunter hurt?" I didn't want Drake to know Charles had spilled the beans.

Pouring more tea into my glass, Drake said, "Josiah, let me ask the questions. Please."

I drank the iced tea and got up to pour myself a

small glass of brandy. I needed it, but my hands were trembling as I poured.

Drake waited until I sat down again. Satisfied I was going to be still for more than a minute, he took out a notebook and a pencil from his pocket, licking the top of the lead. "When did you last see either Hunter or Kathy Wickliffe?"

"It was at Lady Elsmere's birthday party several months ago. Before that, it was at Victoria Weather's party at Haze Corbyn's house."

"Did you speak to them?"

"Just to say hello."

"Nothing else?"

"I had nothing to say to either of them other than superficial pleasantries."

"When Hunter married Kathy, how did you feel?"

I hesitated for a second before answering. I've had enough interviews with the police, knowing to keep my answers short and not lie. Everyone knew or suspected how I felt. "Betrayed. Hurt."

"Enough to kill Kathy?"

"No."

"Your boyfriend walks out on you and marries someone else. You must have been furious."

"Look. Let's cut to the quick. Tell me when Kathy was killed, and I will tell you where I was, so you can rule me out as a suspect."

"Somewhere around eleven last night."

"I played bridge with Lady Elsmere and her friends until about eleven. Then I helped Bess clean up in the kitchen and called it a night around eleven-forty. Now if Kathy was killed at Wickliffe Manor, there is no way I could have driven over there by eleven. It usually takes me about thirty to forty minutes to get to Hunter's house from the Butterfly, depending on the traffic."

In case you didn't know, the Butterfly is my house. It is called that because of the roofline, which shoots upward like the wings of a butterfly. It is a cradle-to-the-grave designed house made of local timber, limestone, and slate. There are no steps in or around the Butterfly, and all the corridors are extra-wide to easily accommodate a wheelchair. The entire back wall is glass—bulletproof because drunken hunters, shooting from across the Kentucky River, keep mistaking my abode for a deer. The look inside and outside the Butterfly is very mid-century. Now you know.

Drake shot a look at Lady Elsmere, who nodded, confirming my alibi.

"Had you ever conversed with Hunter privately after he married?"

"Once, last fall. We ran into each other at the Chevy Chase Inn."

"Was this an accidental meeting?"

"Yes."

"What did you two talk about?"

"He said he was sorry for hurting me, but he was in love with Kathy." That wasn't exactly true, but I didn't want to give Drake further cause to suspect Hunter.

"Do you think they were happy?"

"I have no idea. Ask Hunter."

"Did you like Kathy Wickliffe?"

"I loathed her."

"Did you kill Kathy Wickliffe?"

"No! I've already told you there's no way I could have."

"Did you conspire with anyone to have Kathy Wickliffe killed?"

"No, Detective Drake. I'll swear on the Bible I had nothing to do with Kathy Wickliffe's death, and if you suspect Hunter, forget it. He could never have committed murder. I know the man."

"Really? You didn't know him well enough to realize he would marry a woman he hadn't seen in almost twenty-years."

"That's cruel of you to say, Detective. Everyone knows men are capricious," Lady Elsmere objected.

"Are you going to tell me about Kathy's murder and its location?" I asked, stinging from Drake's remark. "Was she shot, stabbed, run over by a car? Died from the vapors?"

Drake stood and prepared to leave, tucking his notebook and pencil in his coat pocket. "Thank you, ladies. I'll be in touch." He left, closing the library door gently behind him.

Waiting to hear his footsteps echo down the marble hallway, I turned to Lady Elsmere. "I can't stand the man. Why does Drake have to be so adversarial?"

"It's his job, Jo."

"He's a pain in the ass."

Lady Elsmere tisked-tisked, "Such language."

I pursed my lips. "Oh, I've heard you say much worse."

"I'm entitled. Ancient grand dames may speak their minds at anytime."

"What do you know about this?" I asked, really annoyed.

"Drake wouldn't tell me anything either. Just that he couldn't get hold of you and needed to reach out."

"I've turned the ringers off my phone. I didn't want to talk with anyone for a couple of days."

"It looked suspicious."

"Not if Drake had attended your bridge game yesterday. Your friends are vicious."

"Yes, they are—as you say—vicious, but they are fountains of information, innuendos, and observations."

"You mean they are gossips."

"Precisely," answered Lady Elsmere, lighting up a cigarette from a pack she hid in the couch seat cushions.

"Is there anyone they wouldn't trash?" I grabbed

the cigarette from her mouth and the pack, throwing them both into the fire. Lady Elsmere always had a fire in the library, regardless of the season. I was sweating again.

The elderly woman pouted. "You're no fun."

"You pull out the cigarettes around me because you want to create a fuss. You know I won't let you smoke them. If you really wanted a ciggy, you would have waited until I had left."

"Then pour me a bourbon. I have such few pleasures left in life. You can allow me a drinky-poo at least."

"You're such a drama queen."

Lady Elsmere patted the place beside her on the couch. "Let's talk seriously for a moment, Josiah."

"Okay, June," I replied, handing her the drink. FYI—I call Her Ladyship, Lady Elsmere in public, but June in private. She was just June Webster, daughter of a sharecropper, who married an English lord.

"You will be tempted to seek information from Franklin and perhaps see Hunter. You mustn't do either."

"Why not?"

"Because you will be giving Drake a motive for murder. Drake might think Hunter rid himself of Kathy because he regretted the marriage and wanted to come back to you. You mustn't do anything to cause the police to think you care for the man and that he might still carry the torch for you."

"I don't, and he doesn't."

"You love him. It's plain to see on your face. You are such a terrible liar."

I didn't bother arguing, though I had always thought I was a convincing liar. Sleuthing requires one to be a liar, but I thought Lady Elsmere's advice warranted.

"You know the police will check your phone records. They will interview your friends."

"Yes, I know."

"They will scrutinize you, so you must be careful. If you want to help Hunter, stay away from him, and let the police do their job. They must believe the feelings between the two of you are dead."

"Dead? Ha ha. Funny, June."

Arching her eyebrows, Lady Elsmere gave me a sour look.

Hey you—out there—reading this. You and I both recognize I'm not going to leave this murder alone. Surely, you know me better than that. Don't you?

# 4

I went to bed early as the day's stress was too much. I couldn't sleep, so I turned on an old black and white movie to take my mind off my troubles. It was a noir film about murder, so I turned it off.

Looking at my phone, I saw messages from Franklin, Hunter's brother, Matt, my best human friend, and various other associates all wanting me to spill my guts about Hunter. I would call Franklin and Matt back tomorrow, but the rest of the vultures would have to wait a long time for my return call—if ever. I tossed the phone onto the bed.

Baby plopped his head on the bed, looking at me with his soulful eyes.

"Sorry, Baby. Didn't mean to wake you. I'm restless tonight."

A cat jumped on the bed, which I immediately pushed off. I don't mind letting in Baby's pets—the Kitty Kaboodle—each night, but I minded very much sharing a bed with them. Invariably, I would wake up with one slung across the top of my head and another with its bare fanny right up against my cheek with its tail tickling my nose.

Baby licked the offending cat and grabbed him in his enormous mouth, dropping him back in his own bed. The cat immediately jumped out and ran under my dresser. The games began, as his siblings gave chase.

I would never get to sleep now with all this racket. Annoyed, I sat up in bed, not being able to take my mind off Hunter. My emotions flipped all over the place. I was torn between happiness for Hunter now he was free of Kathy and hoped he would be exonerated. I was also furious that he left me for Kathy. I thought she was unworthy of him, but understood why he married her. It was because of Palley, who Kathy claimed was Hunter's son.

I didn't think Palley and Hunter were related, because they didn't resemble each other. Palley was a descendant from Viking blood, while Hunter had Scotch-Irish ancestry. I begged Hunter to get a DNA test, but he refused. Hunter wanted a child so much he ignored the red flags and rushed into the marriage. If Hunter was really Palley's father, why hadn't Kathy contacted Hunter for child support when the boy was small?

And what were the actual circumstances of Kathy's death? No one could ever make me believe Hunter killed someone unless it was in self-defense. What I needed were facts, but how could I get them? I believed Lady Elsmere was right about my avoiding Hunter. I would only cause him harm if this thing went to trial.

But could I stay away?

# 5

I was getting dressed the next morning when I heard the front door open. Baby went bounding into the great room with enthusiasm, so I knew it wasn't a stranger. Only four people had a key to the Butterfly—Matt Garth, Shaneika Mary Todd and her mother, plus Lady Elsmere.

I quickly buttoned my blouse and put on a pair of sandals before sitting at my vanity to comb my hair.

There was a soft knock on my bedroom door. "Josiah?"

It was Matt. My heart beat faster at the sight of him. I love beautiful things, and Matt was beautiful. He was tall, athletic, had curly black hair, light blue eyes, patrician features, and oozed sexuality. Matt was the complete package—an Apollo leaning against my bedroom door—wearing tight blue jeans and a white cotton shirt with the sleeves rolled up to his elbows. The top three buttons of the shirt were undone, exposing a tuft of black chest hair. He looked like the

40s actor, Victor Mature.

"I guess you're here about Hunter."

"Yep, I've been sent by Franklin."

I stopped brushing my hair and swiveled on my vanity bench. "Drake was at Lady Elsmere's yesterday, giving me the third degree."

"What did you tell him?"

I protested, "Nothing. I don't know anything. I can tell you I'm shocked. There must be some mistake. Hunter couldn't kill anyone."

"It doesn't look good, babe. Come into the living room when you finish dressing, so we can talk." Matt gave me an appraising look. "Jo, you skipped a button."

I looked down and saw I had indeed missed a button, exposing my white utilitarian bra—not my frilly pink or black ones I wear for special occasions.

Why do I always look like a frump around this man?

6

I rubbed foundation on and then painted my lips with pink lipstick. I had pink on the brain.

When I entered the great room, I discovered Matt in the kitchen, rummaging through the refrigerator. He pulled out ham and condiments, making himself a thick sandwich with chips and dill pickles on the side. I looked at my watch. It was nine in the morning.

"Didn't you have breakfast?"

"We are eating on the run. It's been a whirlwind since Kathy was,"—Matt paused—"since Kathy was found."

I sat with Matt at my Nakashima dining table and remained quiet until he had gobbled his sandwich. Noting Matt was still hungry, I rose to cut him a piece of chess pie and pour a tall glass of milk. Not averse to dessert at breakfast myself, I cut a piece as well, though I could hardly taste it because I was so upset.

After Matt finished, I retrieved several beers from the fridge. "Let's go out on the patio. It's such a pleasant morning."

Using the beer as a carrot, I enticed Matt to follow outside. We sat at the patio table near the pool and listened to the birds—Cardinals, Carolina Wrens, Cedar Waxwings, Indigo Buntings, Red-headed Woodpeckers, and Meadow Larks—singing while the Kentucky River flowed a hundred feet below the cliff-side. For the first time, I noticed Matt had dark circles under his eyes, his facial skin looked pinched with a hint of a beard. Looked like Matt hadn't shaved in a few days.

I spoke first. "All Drake told me was Kathy had been murdered the night before. Can you fill me in?"

"Franklin and I know very little ourselves. Hunter called us from the police station and said he was going to be arrested for the murder of Kathy. He wanted a lawyer fast, as he had quit cooperating with them. He felt he was being railroaded."

"When was this?"

"Let me think. It's been such a whirlwind."

"Take your time."

Matt seemed confused and at a loss.

"Let me help you piece together the timeline, Matt. Who found Kathy's body?"

"Palley. He went to the stable to let the horses out into the pastures."

"So, Kathy was discovered in the horse barn?"

Matt nodded his head. "Yes."

"What time was this?"

"About six-thirty. Palley gets up early to tend the horses and then leaves for a job in Versailles. He is usually gone by eight."

"What's his job?"

"He's employed as a car jockey at the service department of a dealership. Palley loves cars, you know."

As it happened, I was going to lend Palley an old car on my property for a demolition derby last summer when we discovered a body in the trunk. That's all I'll say about that. Remember me complaining about stumbling over dead bodies?

"How does he get to work?"

"Hunter bought Palley a fixer-upper. That's his primary mode of transportation. The car's a work in progress."

I started taking notes on the pad I had brought out with me. "Okay. Palley goes into the barn at approximately six-thirty in the morning. Then what?"

"He noticed the horses were skittish, but saw nothing unusual. Palley led the horses to the stable paddock and quickly checked them. Then he filled their water buckets until he found Kathy in the last stall."

"Dead?"

"Quite. Rigor mortis had set in."

"This suggests Kathy's death happened before midnight. Where were Palley and Hunter the night before?"

Matt threw up his hands. "We have no information

about Palley's or Hunter's whereabouts. Hunter is not saying, and Palley is too distraught to give reliable information."

"You said Kathy was in a stall. You mean with a horse?"

"Again, I don't know for sure. Drake refused to tell us any details. I think with a horse, but I can't tell you any more than this."

I puffed air from my cheeks in frustration. This was like pulling teeth. "When did you and Franklin get the call about Kathy and from whom?"

"Palley called around eight after he found his mother. He was very upset. The police had taken both Hunter and him to police headquarters for interviews. Palley wanted us to come down and help."

"Help how? Palley's eighteen now. You wouldn't be able to sit in the interrogation room with him."

Matt snapped, "I'm just telling you what happened, Jo."

"Alright. Alright. I'm just asking. When did Hunter call?"

"Later that afternoon." Matt ran his hand through his thick black hair. "I'm sorry. I didn't mean to bark. Franklin is frantic, and the baby is fussy because she senses something is off."

Matt was living with Hunter's brother, Franklin, because of the baby's childcare issue. The child in question was Matt's daughter, Emmeline. Her mother was Meriah Caldwell, the famous mystery writer, who also had mental health issues, which was why Matt had custody. Since Matt worked long hours as a tax lawyer and Franklin was practically lactating, they joined forces to take care of the baby. Matt dropped the child off at daycare on his way to work, and Franklin picked her up and did the things parents needed to do to care for their offspring—cook dinner, wash clothes, get the baby ready for bed before Matt got home. I hate to say it, since I had my doubts about two men taking care of a baby, but it was a system that worked well. Emmeline was thriving.

"I understand. So Palley called?" I wanted to get back on track.

"Franklin and I rushed to the police department. We were not allowed to see either Hunter or Palley. However, the police made appointments to talk with us."

"You mean today?"

"Yes, later this afternoon, but we're not going."

"Um, I know I wouldn't not show up."

"That's a double negative."

"Matt, the police take a dim view of skipping interviews."

"Here's the fly in the ointment. I will not speak to the police without a lawyer, and neither will Franklin."

"Who did you call?"

"Shaneika Mary Todd. She will represent me, but

not Franklin. She has rescheduled my interview for later this week."

"Let's back up a moment. Why won't she represent Franklin?"

"She refuses to see Hunter, Franklin, or Palley. Says it is a conflict of interest since she is on a retainer from you."

An osprey flew overhead—its shadow preceding a dive to catch a fish.

I leaned back in my chair and sipped my beer. I don't even like beer, but the taste was comforting today. Looking at my notes, I was totally confused. Yep, my head was spinning like a child's top.

There were too many missing pieces of the puzzle. Just too many!

# 7

Matt and I sat quietly for a few moments while Matt finished his beer. Finally, he said, "Jo, I've got a favor to ask."

"What is it? You need money for Hunter's defense?"

"Nothing like that, but I've got to go back to work. I'm in the middle of a big case, and I can't afford to jeopardize my job. I can't deal with Franklin, this murder mess, and the baby all at the same time. Can you take Emmeline for a time, please? Until we get our ducks in a row."

Mind you, I don't object to babysitting Emmeline for several hours here and there, but she walks now. I didn't think I was up to watching a mobile baby 24/7 for days. It was one thing when I could put her into a car seat or playpen, and quite another to chase her around the Butterfly all day long. Besides my farm was a dangerous place for a wandering child—the animals, the farm equipment, the pool, and the cliff—not to mention the bees. But looking at Matt's wishful face, I knew I couldn't turn him down. After all, the man had taken a bullet for me. "Sure. Bring her tomorrow evening. I need a day to childproof the house."

"Thank you. It will give Franklin some time to arrange things for Hunter."

"When will Hunter's arraignment be?"

"The day after tomorrow. Franklin is looking for a lawyer to represent Hunter now."

"Shaneika is the best criminal lawyer in the state. I'm surprised she's using me as an excuse not to represent Hunter. I know she likes him."

"Can you find out why?"

"I'll try, Matt, but you find another lawyer for Hunter for the arraignment in the meantime."

Matt wiped his mouth with the back of his hand before asking, "Are you going to see Hunter?"

"And give the police a motive to kill Kathy? No, I won't have anything to do with him. In fact, Lady Elsmere has already warned me to stay away."

"Do you think she knows something?"

"Honey, she is more plugged in than MI-5 or the FBI. Of course, she knows something, but she won't spill. The old biddy will tell me when she thinks the time is right." I paused for a moment. "Has Hunter asked for me?"

Matt shook his head. "Not that I'm aware. Not even Franklin has spoken with Hunter. I'm sorry, Josiah, but this is all I know. Everything is up in the air."

"Matt, go home and get some rest. You look beat. I'll take Emmeline. Check her off your list. We'll be fine."

The tension drained from Matt's face, and he looked relieved.

I was honored Matt trusted me with his child. I also knew he worried Meriah would hear about the murder case, and the fact Emmeline lived with Franklin, the accused's brother. It might encourage her to seek custody again.

I would help for as long as I was able, but that wasn't what concerned me. I realized a dark secret I had been afraid to admit. Did Hunter really kill Kathy?

I thought it possible, even though I wouldn't voice my opinion out-loud.

It was a thought I would keep hidden in the dark recesses of my mind.

# 8

After Matt left, I changed my clothes into something more suitable for the city. It was warm outside, so I left Baby at home in the air-conditioned Butterfly, much to his chagrin. He loved to ride in the car, or I should say, my vintage Volkswagen van.

It only took me thirty minutes to reach Shaneika Mary Todd's office downtown since traffic was light. I parked and hurried into the elevator up to the third floor, where her office sat right across from it. I went into the main reception room where several people waited with stony-eyed glares, thumbing through their phones. Gee, whatever happened to perusing old magazines and eavesdropping on the receptionist talking on the phone? That's how one picks up actual information. I hated this new techno world.

"Is she in?" I asked, motioning at Shaneika's office door.

The receptionist rose from her desk. "Yes, but she's in with someone."

"That's okay," I replied as I swept into Shaneika's office, shutting the door a little harder than expected.

The receptionist ran in after me, giving Shaneika a worried look. "I'm sorry, but Mrs. Reynolds rushed right in."

"It's okay, Tamara. I'll take it from here," Shaneika said, not even looking up from her brief.

The receptionist narrowed her eyes, giving the lasting impression that she didn't like me at all.

I smiled sweetly at her.

"Sit down, Josiah," Shaneika said.

I plopped into a chair before Shaneika's desk.

"Didn't you see there were other people waiting in the reception room and didn't my receptionist say I was in conference with a client?"

"Client? I don't see any client. Your receptionist always lies where I am concerned. I knew you were free."

Shaneika still hadn't looked up from her brief.

"Why aren't you taking Hunter's case?" I asked.

"And a good morning to you as well."

"Why aren't you taking Hunter's case?" I repeated.

Shaneika finally looked up and took off her reading glasses, flinging them onto the massive desk. "Because if I lose the case, everyone will be angry with me, including my mother, who is very fond of Hunter."

"Is that the only reason?"

"Hunter failed his polygraph test. Showed high deception."

"That's not good." I didn't question how Shaneika knew, realizing she had contacts in the police department.

"No, it is not."

"Matt indicated you would not be representing either Palley, Franklin, or Hunter."

"That's right."

"Because of me?"

"Partly. It would be a conflict of interest."

"Anything else?"

"Hunter hasn't asked me to represent him," Shaneika answered simply.

"Didn't Franklin ask you?"

"Franklin is not Hunter."

I insisted, "You know Hunter did not kill Kathy."

"No, I don't, and neither do you. I've been at this long enough not to make assumptions about any defendant. You'd be surprised what people will do when they are angry, jealous, or fearful."

"Jealous? Was Kathy stepping out on Hunter?"

Shaneika gave a familiar sour look—the one demonstrating I was trying her patience.

"Let me make this simple for you, Shaneika. If Hunter asks, take the case. I'm firing you as my attorney."

Ignoring my statement and not looking in the least bit concerned, Shaneika asked, "Have the police talked with you?"

"Did you hear me? I'm firing you."

"Yes, I heard you, Josiah. As usual, I let your comments go in one ear and out the other. Now—have the police interviewed you?"

"Detective Drake cornered me yesterday at Lady Elsmere's home."

"What did you tell him?"

"Not much. There wasn't anything to tell. Except at social functions, I haven't had contact with Hunter since he married Kathy."

"Whatever you do, don't lie to the police."

"I know they are probably chasing my phone records as we speak."

"That's what I would do if I were Drake. The best thing you can do for Hunter is stay far away. Understand?"

I nodded. "That's what Lady Elsmere suggested."

"She's right. Now, go about your merry way, Josiah. I've got work to do."

"Won't you even help at Hunter's arraignment?"

"I plan to go to the courthouse and sit in. That's all I can do at the moment."

"What time is his hearing?"

"None of your beeswax, Miss Busybody. Get out and stay away. You'll just mess up the works."

I got up to leave.

Leaning back in her chair, Shaneika asked in a soft voice, "Josiah, just one thing. Did you kill Kathy?"

"Shaneika, I can honestly say my hands are clean. Hate your hair, by the way." I replied before blowing a kiss while heading out the door.

Every time I saw Shaneika Mary Todd—a descendant of the famous Todd-Lincoln family, albeit on the wrong side of the blanket—she had a different hairstyle. This time she had her hair straightened and cut into a bob. It made her look like a stuffy matron and not the fierce African-American criminal defense attorney so feared she made hardened detectives and Yale law grads quake in their shoes.

You ask why I need a criminal lawyer on retainer. Well, ask away. I'm not telling on myself. I'm pleading the Fifth.

# 9

I made a quick stop at the bank and hurried over to Walter Neff's office. Walter Neff was a shady private detective who had worked with me on several cases. He could ferret out the tiniest of details. Better yet, he was totally lacking in scruples and for a dollar would sell his own mother down the river. Walter once tried to kill me over a lottery ticket, but that's another story. Yep, he's another man who tried to kill me. It's a long list.

Did I trust Walter? I trusted his greed, and that's how I could control him.

Walking into his plush office, I found short, balding, pudgy Walter clipping his toenails while puffing on a big stogie.

Lovely. I'm being facetious here in case you didn't know.

Walter looked up in surprise. "Don't you ever knock?"

"Where's your staff?"

"I've got one girl, and she's out to lunch."

I looked at the clippings on the floor and hoped he wouldn't *his girl* to clean the mess up. "Really, Walter! Clipping your toenails in your office is disgusting."

"I'm on my lunch break, too. How did you get in? The front office door was supposed to be locked."

"I guess your little old assistant forgot."

"Come back in thirty minutes."

"I can't understand you with that cigar in your mouth."

"I said, 'Come back in thirty minutes.'"

"What?"

"Come back later."

"What?" I put my hand up to my ear. "What did you say?"

Realizing I was hassling him, Walter pulled the cigar from his mouth. "Whaddya want, Josiah?"

"I want to hire you to investigate Kathy Wickliffe's murder."

Walter smirked. "No can do, Toots. I'm working for the district attorney on that case."

"That's all the better. You'll have the inside track."

"Unethical. No way."

I smiled. "Since when have ethics mattered to you?" I pulled ten crisp one-hundred-dollar bills from my pocket and laid them out one by one on his desk.

Walter eyed them the way Baby eyed a strip of bacon.

"All I want is a little information now and then. I want to know why Hunter was arrested. How was Kathy murdered?"

Walter reached for the ten bills, but I swooped up five of them. "I'll give you the rest when you deliver."

"I want five hundred on top of the thousand."

That's the Walter Neff I know and love. I agreed. "Deal. Now start smacking your gums."

"This never came from me. Understand, Jo."

"I know the drill, Walter. Let's start with how Kathy was killed."

"Kathy Wickliffe died of blunt-force trauma. The back of her head was caved in."

"Where did this happen?" I didn't want to tip Walter off that I already knew some details—just in case he lied.

"The forensic boys think a struggle began in the barn aisle near the west entrance where she was killed, and then dragged into a stall."

"Which stall?"

"The one on the left facing west."

"How was her body situated?"

"On her back."

"Defensive wounds?"

"Yeah. There were abrasions on her face and hands. The barn was torn up. She had been fighting with someone."

"But you said Kathy had been hit from behind."

"The po-po think she turned to flee when she received the fatal blow."

"What about blood evidence?"

"There was blood on the aisle floor, the stall door, and the straw bedding inside the stall. They're still testing."

"DNA?"

"Results haven't come in yet."

I was puzzled. "I don't understand. If the police are still collecting evidence, why was Hunter arrested?"

Neff smirked. "Because, my dear Josiah, Hunter Wickliffe confessed he murdered his wife!"

# 10

"HE CONFESSED?!" I shrieked.

"Yes, Toots, he blew the polygraph test and when confronted by Detective Drake, Hunter said he murdered his wife. Sang like a bird."

I protested, "I don't believe it."

"Believe it."

"I think he is lying."

Walter made a face.

"What? You think Hunter killed Kathy?"

"My job has been to interview friends and families concerning the activities of Kathy. I'm still interviewing. As soon as my *girl* comes back, I'm going out to interview more folks."

Walter was a throwback to the past where women were called girls, dames, skirts, or dolls. Wait a minute—if women were over thirty-five, biddy was a word often used. He called women Toots or Honey if he liked them. See what I mean. Luckily, Walter liked me—sort of.

I replied, "Obviously you are finding out stuff about Kathy."

"Let me put it this way. I probably would have killed her if she had been my wife."

"Well, that's not reassuring. Look, Walter. Hunter doesn't kill his wives. He divorces them. I can give you his exes' phone numbers, and you can talk to them. They are still friendly with the man. The only bad thing they would say about Hunter is that he was never home. His mistress was work."

"If they are not on my list, I don't talk to them."

"You don't want to see an innocent man go to jail, do you?"

"I don't think Hunter is innocent."

Walter was a sharp cookie. It was upsetting to see him believing Hunter was guilty.

"Okay, tell me what you've got on Kathy. What did she do to make Hunter so angry he would kill her?"

"What haven't I got on that dame—extortion, blackmail, and fraud."

I didn't like Kathy and thought she was sketchy, but blackmail and fraud? Didn't think that about her, but I was curious to learn what Walter had on her. "Looks like little petite Kathy has been a busy girl. Details, Walter. I need details about our Kathy."

"She married three times not including Hunter—each time upgrading, only the third time, Kathy didn't bother getting a divorce."

I let that sink in for a moment. Finally, I asked, "You mean her marriage to Hunter wasn't legal?"

"Took you a while to catch on."

"Did Hunter know?"

Walter shrugged.

"Has Hunter been told?"

"How would I know?"

"You'd better find out if you want that extra thousand. Tell me more, Walter."

The front door slammed. Walter immediately put out his cigar and pulled on his socks and shoes.

"Yahoo. I'm back." A peroxide blond with a clinched waist and ample bosom entered Walter's office with a large Diet Coke and a sandwich box.

I almost laughed out loud, but restrained myself. Good Lord, she was a cliché right out of a Raymond Chandler novel. I imagined her name was Trixie or Margie—some name ending in 'i.e.'

Spying me, she said, "Oh, I'm sorry, Mr. Neff. I didn't realize you had a client." She put the drink and box on Walter's desk.

"Don't worry, honey. Mrs. Combs was just leaving."

I sighed with relief that Walter had given a false name. The last thing I wanted was a witness who could testify I was bribing the DA's shamus. Giving a quick glance at the desk, I noticed the five one-hundred-dollar bills were missing.

Walter patted his waistcoat, letting me know the

money was safely tucked on his person. *Trixie* had seen nothing to incriminate us.

"Yes, I was just leaving. Mr. Neff has agreed to work on a missing person's case for me." Turning to Walter, I warned, "You will be discreet, won't you, Mr. Neff?"

Walter rose from his chair. "We are always discreet, aren't we, Louise?"

Louise nodded emphatically.

"Let me walk you to the door," Walter said, pointing to the back door in his office. "Thank you, Louise. That's all."

So Louise was her name. A nice name for a steady woman. I liked it, as it was my middle name as well.

Louise got the hint and went into the reception room, closing the door on her way out.

Walter pushed me along. "Now don't come here again. When I find out more, I'll contact you. Get along, Toots. Next time I see you, you'd better have lots of Benjamins for me, and you can throw in a few of his cousins as well." He opened the back door of his office and shoved me into the hallway.

I turned to say something, but he shut the door in my face.

I guess that was that—for now.

# 11

I went home to prepare the Butterfly for Emmeline by rolling out the high chair, playpen, and crib, which I stored in Asa's bedroom. Asa is my grown daughter in case you didn't know.

I put the high chair and playpen in the great room with the crib in my bedroom. It took me twenty minutes to secure all my art glass, like my Stephen Powell pieces, on Asa's bed. I then locked her bedroom door and went into the kitchen. I already had child-proof locks on all the lower cabinets and drawers, followed by stowing away knives on the countertops. Once that was done, I found Emmeline's sippy cup, special plate, and silverware, giving them all a good washing.

Realizing something was up, Baby followed, sniffing at every lock and looking up at me expectantly. He followed from room to room, helping to install electrical protective plugs. After an hour of plugging and putting delicate art objects away from greedy baby hands, I locked every nonessential room. Doubtless, I had forgotten something, but that was all my brain could fathom at the moment. I needed a sit-down.

I poured a glass of sweet iced tea and went out onto the patio.

I gasped.

There it was, staring at me. Oh, my gosh—the pool! How could I forget the pool? I made a mental note to lock all the entrances to the house. I went back inside and wrote large notes—LOCK DOORS TO POOL—and taped them to the patio glass doors. The pool was my single biggest worry. Every year there was a story of a toddler unlocking doors and drowning in the family pool. The thought of such a thing happening filled me with dread.

"Baby, you're gonna have to help keep an eye on Emmeline. I can't do it all by myself."

Realizing I didn't want the responsibility of watching a baby for days, I pouted. I had an adult routine which I enjoyed, and a toddler messed with my schedule. Selfish, I know, but I knew Matt and Franklin needed help, so I would lend a hand. It's what friends do for one another.

Looking at my watch, I noticed it was near suppertime. I heated some leftover stew and sat down at my Nakashima table to eat while watching birds through the glass windows as they snacked on suet at the feeding stations. It would be the last meal I would enjoy for some time as babies were fussy eaters and notoriously kept the adults from enjoying their grub.

The doorbell jolted me out of my reverie. Sighing, I glanced at my watch and reluctantly put down my spoon. Franklin was early. I hurried to the front double doors and threw them open.

There stood Franklin with his arms full of baby accouterments. He pushed past me and, upon seeing the playpen, dumped everything into it. "Josiah, help me get Emmeline's stuff out of the car."

"There's more?"

"Her suitcases. Get her suitcases, and I'll bring her in."

"There's more than one suitcase? How long is Emmeline staying?" I asked, trying to tone down my frantic timbre.

"Would you get her diaper bag, too? Oh, don't forget the boxes of diapers in the back." Franklin rushed back to Matt's Mercedes. I should have guessed he would have used Matt's car as Franklin's Smart Car could barely hold two passengers.

Franklin took Emmeline from her car seat and disappeared into the Butterfly while I struggled with the diaper bag and several large boxes of diapers. It wasn't easy.

"Do you still have a car seat?" Franklin asked, rushing past to get more boxes of diapers.

"I put it in the van yesterday. Emmeline will be fine."

"I better check it before I leave."

"Whatever makes you happy, Franklin." I wasn't going to argue with an anxious papa.

I dumped the bag and diaper boxes in the foyer before searching for Emmeline. Franklin had put her in the playpen along with her things. She gave a bewildered look and promptly started crying.

Baby immediately went over, pressing his nose against the playpen mesh, upon which Emmeline grabbed Baby's nose. I immediately picked her up and said, "No, Emmeline. Be gentle with Baby." With Emmeline perched on my hip, I scattered some of her toys on the floor and put her down to play.

Franklin came back some ten minutes later. "Okay. Everything's out of the car. I checked the car seat in the van and made a few adjustments."

"You know I raised a child of my own in this very house, Franklin."

"Is the floor washed? You put her down on the slate. I always put a blanket down first. Floors are dirty."

"Emmeline is fine. See, Baby is lying beside her."

Franklin winced. "He's gonna get her dirty."

"Calm down, Franklin. I have a washing machine and a bathtub to clean away all signs of dog yuck. She'll be spic and span when you take her home again. When will that be?" I know I'm not very subtle.

"You'll never leave her for a second when she gets her bath?"

"Yes, I'm going to leave Emmeline in a bathtub filled with scalding water while I work the bees," I fired back. "How long is she staying?"

Ignoring my question, Franklin plopped down on the couch. "May I have something to drink, please?"

"Sure." I went into the kitchen and poured a glass of iced tea and fixed a plate of molasses cookies. "Here you go."

Franklin grabbed some cookies. "I haven't had anything to eat most of the day. It's been rush, rush, rush."

"How did Hunter's arraignment go?" I asked.

"He pleaded *not guilty*."

"That's good to hear."

"Hunter was denied bail."

I was surprised to hear that. "On what grounds?"

"The DA considered Hunter a flight risk because of his connections in Europe."

"All the court had to do was take away Hunter's passport."

"The judge agreed with the DA. I think they want to make an example out of Hunter since he worked with the courts so often."

"That's why Hunter shouldn't be in jail. Eventually, he's going to run into someone he helped put away."

Franklin nodded. "Shaneika was there."

"Acting as his lawyer?"

"No, but she went to Hunter's public defender lawyer and gave him advice of what to do next."

"Which was?"

"Have the Appellate Court review the bail decision or seek a writ of habeas corpus for the circuit court to review the district court's bail decision. Either way will take time though."

"Did Shaneika say she'll take Hunter's case now?"

"I'm not so sure Hunter wants Shaneika. There's the matter of payment. Shaneika is awfully expensive, and Hunter just doesn't have the money. He's poured all his savings into the farm and the house. Of course, Kathy got her claws into what was left."

"Don't say such things."

Franklin protested, "But it's true."

"It gives Hunter a motive."

Franklin blew air from his cheeks in frustration. I could tell he was exhausted.

"Can Matt help?"

"I can't ask him to do more. Matt is already going through Hunter's financials and coming up with a plan. In addition, he's taken over the farm's invoices and payment of notices, making sure Hunter stays up-to-date on incoming money and stays solvent."

"I see. What's going on with Palley? Has he visited Hunter?"

"Palley went to stay with one of Kathy's exes. As far as I know, Hunter and Palley haven't spoken to each other."

"All Hunter wanted was a son, and the one he

sought may now deny him. It's such a tragedy."

"I know. I can't believe Palley would even think Hunter would harm his mother."

Watching Emmeline's interaction with Baby, I inquired, "What about the horses and the cattle?"

"I'm going out to check on them after I leave here. I'm going to stay at Wickliffe Manor for a few days until I can get help with the animals."

I must have looked skeptical because Franklin objected, "I grew up on a farm. I know how to take care of livestock. I'm hurt that you doubt me so."

Ignoring Franklin's pouting, I ruminated, "They're letting the animals back into the stable?"

"The horses have been out in the pastures since the murder. Luckily, the weather has been good. I was told the police should be finished with the stable this morning."

"Yeah, but you've got to get the animals off that rich grass. Too much sugar."

"No problem with the pregnant mares. They need the nutrients, but the pleasure horses were put in the dry paddock with hay. I know what I'm doing, Jo."

"I'm sorry, Franklin. I think everyone is jumpy about this. You'll feel better when the farm is taken care of, and a defense lawyer is chosen for Hunter. Things will fall into place. You'll see."

Of course, I wasn't so sure of that myself.

"What time is it?" Franklin asked.

"Getting close to six."

"I'd better go. Want to get settled in before night-fall."

I wanted to ask if Hunter had inquired about me, but didn't dare. Maybe it was better not to know.

Since Emmeline was playing with one of her toys, Franklin slipped away without her noticing. I'm sure the crying jag would start the moment she discovered he was gone.

I felt a crying jag coming on myself.

Emmeline and I could blubber together.

Perfect.

# 12

I woke up with a headache.

The night had been an exercise in drama. Once Emmeline got over the shock of being left with me, she tormented Baby, whose only crime was that he was trying to be a good host. I admonished her for pulling his tail or ears or hitting him with her stuffed teddy bear. She didn't grasp the concept that people, including toddlers, do not hit animals. It was surprising, as she had never exhibited aggressiveness toward Baby before. They had always been the best of buds.

I finally put her to bed in my room, but sleep for her and relief for me didn't come for a long time.

She cried.

I wept.

Baby whimpered.

We all finally drifted into blessed sleep until I awakened the next morning. The room was quiet.

Good. Maybe I could shower and dress while Emmeline still slept. I needed a few moments to myself. I glanced at the crib.

EMMELINE WAS NOT IN HER BED!

I sat up. Oh, my Lord—the pool! I swear my heart stopped until I realized she couldn't have gotten far as I had locked the bedroom door.

Then I heard a giggle. A giggle?

I leaned over the bed and spied Emmeline and Baby snuggling together like two peas in a pod in Baby's bed. The Kitty Kaboodle were in various positions around the two, with one lying on top of Emmeline's head and another cat with its fanny against Emmeline's cheek. The sight of the kitties doing to Emmeline what they like to do to me gave much satisfaction. I took a picture of them all in Baby's bed. I planned to show it to Franklin when he annoyed me again. The fact that one cat had its fanny against Emmeline's cheek would keep him up at night.

Happy to have frightened me near to death, Emmeline gave a jubilant smile and held out her arms.

"Oh, you little scamp!" I cooed, picking her up. Giving Emmeline a hug, I sniffed—unconsciously and impulsively. There was an unpleasant odor of stale milk, dog, and poo about her.

"Well, I see a bath and diaper change are in order. Let's get breakfast over first and then have a nice bath and a fresh change of clothes." I was speaking more about myself, rather than the baby.

I fed the cats and Baby out on the patio before giving Emmeline cereal and a sippy cup of milk. She knocked the sippy cup to the floor and proceeded to turn her bowl upside down. However, a lot of the cereal remained on the high chair tray. I picked up a toasted oat and popped it in my mouth. Emmeline watched and got the idea. She acted as if this was something new to her, but I'm sure Matt went through this same routine every morning.

I finished the rest of the molasses cookies and drank from the sippy cup which I plucked off the floor.

Emmeline threw cereal at me.

Yep. It was going to be a great day.

# 13

Two days came and went. Matt and Franklin called each night, but I wouldn't let them speak to Emmeline. It would just start a crying jag—mostly from me being stuck with this kid. The person I wanted to hear from was Walter Neff, but he didn't call, and I didn't dare call him. There must be no record of us having had contact, so I went about my business getting honey ready for the state fair honey contest. It was a very competitive event where beekeepers from all over the state submitted their honey for judging. I always started weeks earlier to get six jars of honey ready. There could be no microscopic wax, hairs, bee parts, or pollen in the honey, so I filtered it with my fancy-dancy ultra filter. It takes days for the honey to strain through. Many beekeepers used magnifying glasses and straws to get out non-honey debris.

Now with honey for sale, we leave such stuff in. It's not visible to the customer's eyes, but some buyers ask for honey with debris such as pollen because they think it is healthier. I don't argue. I just sell honey with a grin and take the customer's money.

The fair was in a few weeks, and I wanted to add to my already impressive collection of ribbons. When I display the ribbons at the farmers' market, my honey sales go up. Of course, I lord it over the other beekeepers at the market. Yeah, I can be that way.

There is another beekeeper who keeps lowering his prices at the market, and it has cut into my sales. I bought and tasted his honey early in the spring and found it tasted odd. I think he is feeding his bees corn syrup instead of letting them forage for nectar—a big no-no from me. Corn syrup is not good for bees, but they will happily eat it with abandon.

When you buy cheap honey, you get a crappy product—and never buy honey from grocery stores. Always buy from a local beekeeper. Enough on that subject.

The phone rang. I didn't answer as I had my hands full with cleaning Emmeline. Oh, Lordy, when was Matt going to pick her up? I was getting too old to take care of a baby.

Baby contributed to the cleaning process by licking her.

"Baby, stop it! You're getting dog goo on her," I scolded, frustrated that I had to wipe Emmeline's skin down again. I finally got the baby slobber free and into her little sunflower outfit.

With Emmeline safely ensconced in her playpen, I

went over to my landline phone and clicked on the answering machine.

"Mrs. Reynolds? My name is Eli Bradley, and I am defending Hunter Wickliffe. I would like to make an appointment for an interview. I understand you and Mr. Wickliffe were close at one time, and I need some background information before the preliminary hearing convenes. Please call me back at 502 555-xxxx."

I immediately called Shaneika on her private number.

"What's up?" she said, answering it.

"I got a call from an Eli Bradley who said he is defending Hunter. What gives?"

"I told you that Hunter didn't want me. Bradley is an excellent lawyer. Very bright. He'll do right by Hunter."

"If he's so good, why haven't I heard of him?"

"He's from Louisville. Look—I'm due in court right now. Cooperate with Bradley. I've worked with him on several cases. He's first-rate, so don't badger him."

"Who—moi?"

Shaneika hung up.

Drat! I reluctantly called this man back.

"Hello?"

"Mr. Bradley, this is Josiah Reynolds. I'm returning your call."

"Very unusual name for a woman."

"Yeah, it's a riot."

"I would like to schedule an interview, please."

"You will have to come to my place. I've got a baby on my hands."

"Yes, Franklin Wickliffe said you were taking care of his baby while he settled a few things."

I thought—*his baby!* What nerve.

"I'll be here all day. Just come anytime." I gave Bradley the gate code and hung up.

I looked down at my clothes. I was wearing another stained T-shirt and cut-off britches. I hadn't even combed my hair yet. Not exactly the outfit one dons for a meeting with a defense lawyer. Since I didn't trust Emmeline to stay in her playpen as she proved to be an escape artist from her crib, I called the Big House.

I begged Amelia, Lady Elsmere's nurse, to take care of Emmeline for a few hours while I freshened up. She drove a hard bargain, but we finally agreed on fifty dollars for two hours.

DEAL!

# 14

I showered, washed and dried my hair, and dressed in clean clothes. Looking in the mirror, I saw a respectable middle-aged woman. Now for some powder and lipstick.

Uh-oh, the doorbell rang. I looked at my watch.

The lawyer was early.

I hurried to the front door hoping it was Eli Bradley, as I wanted to get this interview over.

It was.

"Mr. Bradley?"

"Greetings, Mrs. Reynolds. I hope I've come at a good time."

"May I see some ID please?"

"Of course." He pulled out his wallet while I studied him, catching whiffs of his expensive cologne.

Mr. Bradley was a man about my age and a little over six feet. His thick brown hair contoured into a widow's peak above the forehead, and the hair near his temples was turning gray. The look of his widow's peak and arched eyebrows over his hazel eyes accentuated by long eyelashes gave Mr. Bradley a beguiling air. Wearing an expensive navy suit with a blue and gray striped silk tie, Mr. Bradley looked respectable, well-to-do, and healthy—no signs of being a drinker or user of recreational drugs. I can spot those a mile away with their rheumy eyes and florid skin.

I was determined not to like him. Don't ask me why.

He showed me his driver's license.

"Come in, please. We'll go in here." I led him from the foyer to the great room.

Bradley stood, gazing at the room with its paintings. "I can see you are an art lover."

"I used to be an art history professor at UK."

"So I've been told."

"By whom?"

"May I sit?"

So, he was going to ignore my question. Okay—be that way. "Yes, please."

"Who is that?" Bradley demanded, spying Baby on the patio peering through the glass at us. "I love dogs."

The statement made me feel a bit friendlier towards Bradley.

"That is Baby, my English Mastiff."

"I would love to meet him."

"Mr. Bradley, he would get saliva all over your nice suit. He's fine outside."

"Maybe another time then." Bradley looked about. "Where is the human baby?"

"What?"

"You said you were watching a baby. I assumed it was human."

"Next door at the Big House."

"Oh, I see." Bradley sat across from me and pulled a tape recorder from his briefcase.

I quickly spat out, "I'm sorry, but you can't use that. I refuse to allow it."

"Okey-dokey. May I take notes?"

"Fine," I replied, nodding.

He retrieved a yellow legal pad and a pen from his case. "Can you state your full name for me, please?"

"Josiah Louise Reynolds."

"Your age?"

"Fifty-four."

"Can you state your relationship with Hunter Wickliffe?"

"We were partners."

"How so?"

"We worked together on murder cases."

"Were you romantically involved?"

"Yes."

"Did you think the relationship was headed toward marriage?"

I snorted. "I hadn't thought that far ahead, but probably not. My marriage with my late husband hit a very bad patch at the end, and it left an unpleasant taste in my mouth. Marriage was never spoken of with Hunter as far as I can remember."

"Your first husband, Brannon—he left you for a younger woman and had a child with her," Bradley stated matter-of-factly.

I blinked. "My, my, you have been a busy boy."

"It's my job. I can see how your husband's betrayal would put you off marriage."

"With Hunter having been married three times before, I wasn't sure a fourth time would be any better." I refrained from revealing my health was a major concern. I never told Hunter my kidneys were going south because of the cliff fall some years back. I didn't want to saddle him with a sick wife.

I continued, "I met one of his ex-wives when she came to visit. Lydia was a lovely woman, as I'm sure his other wives were as well. Hunter never said an ill word against any of them."

"But all three of his wives bled him dry."

"It's true Hunter had to start over financially when he came back to the states. I think he felt guilty after the demise of each marriage, as he was at fault. He worked all the time and was never there for them. He thought money would soothe their anger."

"You said you and Hunter worked together on murder cases. What does that mean? You're not an officer of the courts or a law enforcement officer."

"I helped Hunter track down clues."

"Are you trained to do so?"

"Not officially, but I have a knack for solving murders, and I'm very good at sizing up people unless I'm married to them. Ask anyone."

"I have." Bradley scribbled on his notepad.

I wondered with whom he had spoken and what they had said about me.

Bradley asked, "What caused the two of you to call it quits?"

"Hunter rekindled his romance with Kathy. She was his high school flame. She came back into town with her son, Palley, after her latest divorce, and that was all she wrote."

"So he cheated on you?"

"Hunter and I never said we were going steady. It was a little more complicated, which I'm sure you already know."

"You mean about Palley?"

I nodded.

"Do you think Palley was Hunter's son?"

"No."

"Why?"

"Because they look nothing alike."

"Did you caution Hunter to get a paternity test?"

"Yes."

"And?"

"I have no idea if he had or not. Are you going to

insist Hunter do one now?"

"The DA will probably get a court order for one. Surely you can see if Hunter is not the biological father of Palley, it gives Hunter a motive."

I looked over at Baby, who whined and pawed the glass of my floor-to-ceiling back windows.

Bradley followed my gaze. "Did you like Kathy Wickliffe?"

"You've got to be kidding me. The woman was looking for a meal ticket."

"I guess that means no."

"It means no with a capital *NO*."

"Did Mr. Wickliffe rekindling his relationship with Kathy make you angry? Did the thought of another man abandoning you cause a blazing hate for Kathy Wickliffe? Maybe enough to hurt her?"

I gave pause at Bradley's use of the word *abandoning*. "I despised the woman, but not enough to kill her. If I were to kill someone, it would have been Hunter."

Bradley wrote furiously on his notepad. Maybe I shouldn't have spoken about killing Hunter.

I quickly added, "Pump your brakes, Mr. Bradley. I see where this is going. You're looking for 'someone else killed Kathy Wickliffe' defense. It wasn't me. I have an ironclad alibi."

Bradley gave a hint of a smile.

I figured Bradley had already talked to Lady Elsmere. "Look, I had many emotions concerning this marriage. I thought Hunter and I were rock solid. I was surprised, then mystified, then angry, but I understood why Hunter married Kathy. In the end, I wished Hunter well."

"You said you understood why Hunter married Kathy. Why so?"

I hesitated. I didn't want to give anyone ammunition for a motive. "Guess he loved her."

Bradley gave a thoughtful look. "I know this must be trying for you, but the prosecution will undoubtedly subpoena you. I must know what you will say under oath."

"This is off the record. I don't want you to even write it down."

Bradley put down his pen. "Shoot."

"Look at Kathy's exes. There are also problems with the law in her past."

"Yes, but Mr. Wickliffe confessed to the murder."

"And then pleaded *not guilty* at the arraignment. Hunter's not thinking of changing his plea to *guilty*, is he?"

"Mr. Wickliffe hasn't advised me of such, but I think he should make a plea deal."

"If Hunter has pleaded *not guilty*, he's going to fight the charges. Are you going to get the confession thrown out?"

"I'll try, but all the evidence points to his guilt."

"Yes, but you won't tell me why except he confessed?"

"I can't comment, except to say this is going to be a Hail Mary strategy."

"Will there be a grand jury?"

"Only a preliminary hearing is necessary for murder, but I will request a grand jury to push the trial date back farther. I want to draw this case out as long as possible. At the moment, I have no defense. But the DA will decide whether Mr. Wickliffe goes before a preliminary hearing or the grand jury."

"When is the preliminary hearing?"

"Next week. I would advise you not to attend and to stay away from Hunter Wickliffe period."

"Understood."

"The fact that you are taking care of my client's niece will only draw attention to you and Hunter."

"If you knew about Emmeline, why ask if she was here?"

"To see if you told the truth. Attorneys will ask questions even when they know the answer. It's to determine how a witness might respond on the witness stand."

"Emmeline has no biological connection to Hunter or his brother, Franklin. I did Franklin's roommate a favor while they straightened things out. Matthew Garth and I go way back—even before I met Franklin or his brother. Hunter's arrest has thrown their household into a tizzy. The two live together for the baby's sake."

"I'm just saying, everybody knows everything about everyone in this town. Anything you do will get out eventually."

"Then pack your bags for Louisville if you're not up to it."

Bradley shot an unsympathetic glance in my direction while gathering his pen and pad, stuffing them in his briefcase. "I think we're done for now, but I will probably need to interview you again. Thank you for allowing me to speak with you, Mrs. Reynolds." He stood and walked toward the front door.

I followed.

Bradley turned and remarked, "Sometime soon I'd like to meet your mastiff. I love dogs, and I've never petted an English Mastiff. Two hundred pounds?"

"There about."

He shook my hand, opened the door, and left in a rented light blue Bronco.

I just didn't know what to think about his visit. I was quite perplexed.

Did I help Hunter, or did I give Eli Bradley ammunition for Hunter to make a plea deal, causing the man to spend the rest of his life in prison?

# 15

Franklin called later that afternoon and stated he was coming to pick Emmeline up. Thank the Lord! He found us in the pool, along with Baby, enjoying an afternoon swim.

As soon as Emmeline saw Franklin, she threw out her arms and cooed in utter delight.

I carried her out of the pool.

"I see I won't have to give you a bath tonight," Franklin teased, kissing Emmeline on the cheek and top of her sunhat.

"Let me give her a quick shower, Franklin. I want to get the chlorine off her skin. You can get Emmeline's clothes ready."

Franklin and Baby followed me into my bedroom.

I jumped into the shower with a persnickety Emmeline, because now she wanted Franklin. A moment later, we came out, and I handed a towel-wrapped Emmeline to Franklin. I went back in the bathroom to shower.

"I hope Emmeline wasn't any trouble," Franklin called out to me.

"She was a peach," I lied, while taking a quick shower in my bathing suit. Giving a peek in the mirror, I could see the beginning of sunburn. Great. With my red hair and now reddening skin, I would look like a walking tomato.

Franklin had already diapered and dressed Emmeline in a cotton bunny-printed jumper when I appeared again. He was trying to put socks on, but Emmeline hampered the process, scooting across my bed, giggling. Franklin grabbed a chubby leg and pulled her back. When he reached for the other sock, she scooted across the bed again, delighting in this new game.

Baby's persistent barking added to the pandemonium.

"Be quiet, Baby," I admonished, picking up Emmeline and placing her on my lap, upon which she swung around, hitting me in the face.

"You little devil," I remarked, grabbing her flailing arms, which caused her to burst into tears.

"I'm sorry, Jo," Franklin apologized, putting on the other sock and then her shoes quickly. "Emmeline's been aggressive lately. We are hoping it is a phase."

"Are you going to do anything about it?"

"And how do you suggest we temper this behavior with a child that's not even two yet, Miss Know-It-All?"

I didn't reply, since I had a daughter who frequently engaged in violence and loved guns. Maybe my parenting skills weren't spectacular after all.

"Let's feed the rugrat before you go. It's been two hours since she's had something."

"Good idea." Franklin picked Emmeline from my lap, carried, and dropped her into the high chair stationed in the great room.

I gathered animal crackers and the sippy cup filled with milk. "Here you go," I said to Franklin.

He handed the sippy cup to Emmeline, who immediately threw it on the floor with glee. Franklin sighed.

"I'll get it," I groused, retrieving the cup while Franklin put animal crackers on the tray. I picked up a bear cookie and popped it into my mouth.

Emmeline immediately picked up a giraffe and chewed on it. She grabbed another cracker, slipping it to Baby.

I took a fake sip of milk and placed the sippy cup on the tray as well. She didn't throw it this time. I had figured out Emmeline wanted what others coveted. At the moment it was a sippy cup and crackers, but where would it end? A Corvette and a tiara when she was sixteen?

"You got everything settled?" I asked.

Franklin put more animal crackers on the tray. He sat down in one of the Nakashima chairs, as did I. "As much as I could at this stage."

"You going to your apartment or home to Wickliffe?"

"Home to Wickliffe. I'm taking Emmeline with me. Matt will join us on the weekend, and we will decide what to do from here on out."

"Decide on what?"

"Matt's big tax case should be finalized by Friday. If the case is off his plate, Matt will take a few days off. We want to take a breather."

"Decide on what, Franklin?"

"I'm still looking for someone to take care of the horses, but I just can't leave the house alone. I'm afraid someone will break into it if it sits empty."

"What about Palley?"

"What about him? He left Wickliffe Manor the day after his mother died and won't return my calls."

"Do you know where he's staying?"

"I heard through the grapevine he is staying with Kathy's first husband in Versailles. This is the man he is most familiar with and considers his father."

"Are you saying the question of his real parentage has surfaced?"

"I don't know, but it should. I think the crux of this case is about Palley."

"You do know Kathy told Hunter that he was Palley's father?"

"Yes. Hunter accepted it as the gospel. I'm afraid the DA will request a DNA sample from both Hunter and Palley. If Palley didn't know about Kathy claiming Hunter was the biological father, he will soon."

I hesitated, but I had to pose the question—"Do you think deep in your heart that Hunter killed Kathy?"

Franklin looked astonished. "No. He's not the type. Hunter divorces his wives—not murders them."

"That's what I say, but no one has ever lied to him about his child's parentage before."

"Palley's possibly his child—maybe, but don't hold your breath." Franklin turned quiet while feeding Emmeline more crackers.

"If we don't think he killed Kathy, then why did he confess, Franklin?"

"I don't know. He won't talk to me, Jo, except to ask how the farm is doing."

"It would seem he is protecting someone."

Franklin and I both stared at each other until Franklin whispered, "Palley again."

"That's what I was thinking, but why would Palley kill his own mother?"

"It's been known to happen. Hunter has worked on cases where the child has killed a parent."

"Did you see Kathy abuse Palley?"

"Truthfully?"

"Yeah."

"Never. She doted on the boy, and Palley returned her affection. Kathy genuinely loved her son."

"I can find no other explanation for Hunter confessing to a murder he didn't commit if it doesn't involve protecting Palley."

"I know." Franklin returned to feeding Emmeline.

I changed the subject. "How is Hunter doing?"

"Depressed the last time I saw him. I haven't been to the jail for a couple of days. Taking care of horses is a lot of work."

"You're preaching to the choir, Franklin."

"Oh, yeah, you board horses."

"Why don't you ask Charles' grandsons to stay at the house and take care of the horses? The boys would appreciate the money and the opportunity to get out from under their mothers' thumbs."

"I don't know. They are in college, right?"

"They are good boys. Malcolm especially is responsible, but I don't think he could take care of those horses and the house by himself."

"We are down to five. The other owners have pulled their horses out."

"I was just thinking you could return to your apartment and get Emmeline back on her schedule. I don't think I'm up to watching her days on end anymore, Franklin. She wears me out."

Franklin frantically asked, "You mean you never want to watch Emmeline again?"

"That's not what I said. An afternoon here and there or for an emergency. I just can't keep up with her since she started walking. Besides, I'm getting ready for the honey judging at the fair."

Franklin twisted his mouth in consternation. "I know Emmeline is a handful since she's been walking."

"Handful? She's a hellion!"

Franklin chortled.

"Please don't ruin this kid by spoiling her."

"I know. Matt is terrible about it."

"I was referring to you, Franklin."

"Oh." Franklin pouted for a moment. "Well, maybe I indulge her a bit."

"Franklin, I'm tired. Please take Emmeline and leave. I'll walk you out." I lugged Emmeline's things to Franklin's car while he followed with Emmeline.

After strapping the baby in her car seat, he turned and inquired, "Is there a message you wish me to give to Hunter?"

I thought for a moment and then said, "No, thank you."

Franklin looked disappointed. "May I tell him you said hello?"

"No."

"Is this the way you want to play Hunter's incarceration?"

"It is."

"Okay. Just want to say thank you for taking Emmeline."

"Glad I could help. Now leave, Franklin. I need a nap."

Franklin grinned before getting into his Smart Car and leaving.

I watched the car disappear down the dusty gravel driveway as I waved. Exhausted, I went back into the Butterfly and slept the evening away.

When did I get so decrepit I couldn't watch a little child for several days?

It was telling about my frame of mind.

I guess I was getting older.

# 16

I got a letter in the mail with no return address. Usually, I would have thrown it in the trash, but curiosity got the better of me. Good thing I opened it as it was from Walter Neff stating a time and location for a meet at a local state park fishing lake around eleven at night. Since the park had a lodge, I could easily get in without being spotted. I thought Walter was being a little too cloak and dagger but played along. I knew he had a flair for the dramatic.

Later that evening, Baby and I climbed into my van and drove to the park, which looked deserted. I passed the lodge and went directly to the lake. The only people I saw were campers sitting around a fire drinking beer, and a few boats on the water night fishing.

Spying Walter's Avanti at the dock's parking lot, I parked and got into his car. "Really, Walter. This is too much. You could have come to my house."

"I trust you burned the note."

Rolling my eyes, I said, "I know you love playing

secret agent, but this is outrageous."

Walter grumbled, "You wanna hear what I've got to say?"

Reluctantly, I nodded.

"Did you bring money?" Walter's beady eyes turned their attention to my purse.

"Are you wired?" I asked.

"Now who is being paranoid?"

I reached over and patted Walter's torso, felt under the seat and along the dashboard before peering into the backseat of his Avanti.

"May I return the favor?" Walter requested greedily eyeing me.

"Don't even think about frisking me. Let's get on with it."

"Money first."

I handed Walter five one-hundred-dollar bills.

He thrust them into his pocket. "Your boy is going down for capital murder. They've got him dead-to-rights."

My heart pounded. "How so?"

"First, there is the confession."

"Yeah, but he pleaded *not guilty* at the arraignment, thereby basically recanting the confession."

"I interviewed Palley, as did the police."

"And?"

"Palley said the marriage was strained. His mother complained about the lack of intimacy and attention from Hunter."

"Did Palley say why?"

"The boy said he thought Hunter didn't like his mother."

"Palley said that?"

"Palley said Hunter was always polite to his mother and did anything she wanted, but there seemed to be a lack of warmth in his interaction with her."

I retorted, "I know a teenage boy didn't say there was a lack of warmth between the two. What did Palley really say?"

"Hunter made excuses not to be around his mother, slept in a different bedroom, and would interact only if Kathy initiated it. Sounds like your boy was having second thoughts about his marriage."

I croaked, "Quit calling Hunter 'my boy.'"

Walter sneered, knowing he had pushed a hot button. I hated it when he got his digs in.

"What else?"

"The police found Hunter's fingerprints on the murder weapon."

"Which is again?"

"A muck shovel."

"There's a problem with that."

"How so?"

"Of course Hunter's fingerprints would be on the muck shovel or the muck rake or any bucket or any feed sack in the barn. He helped with the horses.

Finding his fingerprints means nothing."

"But only his fingerprints were found."

"Again, a good defense lawyer could shred this evidence to bits. Why just Hunter's fingerprints? Palley's prints should have been on those tools since he took care of the horses in the morning—let them out into the pastures. It makes little sense for *only* Hunter's prints to be on the barn tools. The police have got to have more than this. What's the motive?"

Walter licked his lips. "It seems Hunter had a secret paternity test done on Palley, and the boy is not his son. Kathy died five days after Hunter received the results. Maybe when he found out about Palley, he snapped?"

"I don't care. Hunter would have divorced Kathy. He is not the murdering type."

"The DA thinks she's got a tight case against Hunter. She is going to proceed with the trial. She really wants to nail Hunter, Josiah."

"There's got to be more. There's too much loosey-goosey with the evidence." I grabbed Walter's arm and pinched it. "Are you holding out on me for more money?"

"Ouch! Let go. I'll tell ya, Toots. There's more. I've found evidence of Kathy having an affair while married to Hunter."

I was shocked. Even I didn't think Kathy could be this callous and stupid. "An affair? She and Hunter have only been married eight months! Who with?"

"The DA wants me to keep lookin' into it."

"How do you know Kathy was meeting someone? Could be idle gossip."

"We found receipts for the lodge here."

My first thought was Hunter was seeing someone, but it sounded so unlike him. "Who was the lover?"

"Like I said, I'm tracking him down now."

"Kathy met someone here and kept receipts? Could it have been Palley having a romantic tryst? He's of the age now that he would want privacy if dating."

"Kathy was probably seeing someone from her past or met with someone who works at the park. I want you to go into the lodge and walk about. See if you recognize anyone?"

"You want me to help the DA? Not on your life, Walter. Give me back my money."

Walter pushed my hand away. "No way, Toots. The money is mine."

A realization dawned on me. "Oh, I see. I think it is me you want the clerks to ID. You think Hunter and I were having an affair and met here. Just when I think you couldn't get any sleazier, Walter, you surprise me."

"I have to rule you out as seeing Hunter on the sly. Sorry Toots, but I have to go down every possible avenue. I'm just doing my job."

"Is any of the story true?"

"I'm still checking into it, but I think so. Someone

from Wickliffe Manor was coming to the lodge here and paying for a room."

"Were receipts from this state park really discovered?" I didn't know whether or not to believe this.

Walter nodded.

"Where did you find them, and don't tell me Kathy's sock drawer?"

"Can't say anymore."

"I get it. You found receipts, but you can't tie them to either Hunter, Palley, or Kathy. You're grasping at straws, Walter. Not a good look for you. You know the expression 'when a dog catches a car?'"

Walter didn't respond.

"Your dog got run over." Disgusted, I took a deep breath and let myself out of the car. It was a beautiful night with a soft breeze as the full moon dappled its reflection upon the lake, causing it to glisten, but I was so mad I didn't notice.

"Toots. Toots. Josiah! Don't be angry. I'm doing my job. It's not personal," Walter called after me.

I didn't look back as at the moment I hated Walter.

I also hated Hunter for being in this mess and inadvertently involving me.

Good Lord, he was such a stupid man for being so smart.

# 17

I was upset and confused about my feelings for Hunter. Was he meeting someone at the park lodge? He would be dumb enough to keep the receipts. Yet Kathy had a history of cheating on spouses. That Walter Neff couldn't pinpoint the cheater told me none of the lodge staff could ID Hunter or Kathy.

It could have been paid for over the internet. Still, someone had to walk into the lobby to get the key to the room. Hmm. I'm sure the police would have checked Hunter's phone records and computers taken during the raid. Obviously, they couldn't find a link to Hunter, Palley, or Kathy. Walter said receipts—plural. If the police tied those lodge receipts to either Hunter or Kathy, it would be damning for Hunter. I doubted Hunter and Kathy were meeting there for a little romantic kissy-face if what Palley said about their relationship was true.

Hunter hadn't asked for me, which told me something right there. He was either ashamed, guilty, or didn't give a toss about me anymore. It didn't matter. Eli Bradley would have put the kibosh on our meeting.

I hadn't heard from Matt or Franklin, so I guessed the preliminary hearing went well. No news is good news—right? While waiting for some word, I checked the newspaper, but there was nothing about the case. You'd think the *Herald-Leader* would suck this story dry as it was so juicy. Even *Dateline* was sniffing around.

I needed to go on with my life, so I worked with my honeybees and kept to myself. However, I went to Kathy's funeral visitation. Yes, it was to snoop.

Kathy was laid out at a mom and pop funeral home in Nicholasville, just a few miles from my home on Route 169. Putting on my black dress, red lipstick, and black pumps, I left the house without knowing what I was going to say to Palley. The parking lot was full. While circling the lot, I had time to think of what to say. Oh, good! Someone was leaving and backing out. I snatched their spot with alacrity. One hurdle over.

Relatives, curious onlookers, and old high school friends of Kathy and Palley filled the funeral home. I finally made my way to Palley through the crowd, not knowing how he would receive me.

To my shock, Palley cried excitedly, "Mrs. Reynolds! Mrs. Reynolds!" He grasped my hand while struggling to compose himself, his mouth quivering.

I squeezed his hand. "I know, Palley. This is dreadful."

He nodded and let go. Turning to his right, he blurted, "Mrs. Reynolds. This is my father, Dwight Haskell."

Unaware of my astonishment, Palley chatted, "This is Mrs. Reynolds. She was going to give me an old car for the demolition derby last year, Dad."

I hoped the shock didn't show on my face. "Sorry to meet you under such circumstances, Mr. Haskell." I had stumbled upon an older version of Palley—blond hair, blue eyes, high cheekbones, tall—in other words—both Palley and Mr. Haskell were from Viking stock. I had discovered Palley's real biological father!

And I'm sure Mr. Haskell recognized my realization.

# 18

Dwight Haskell shook my hand, but his eyes weren't friendly. "I understand you befriended Palley. It was nice of you to offer him a car."

"Unfortunately, it didn't work out, but I'm glad to know Palley finally got a vehicle for the demolition derby."

"Yeah, about that. I understand you found a body in the car."

Palley interjected, "I told you it wasn't Mrs. Reynolds' fault, Dad."

"You were Hunter Wickliffe's girlfriend, weren't you?"

"Yes, Mr. Haskell. I was."

"So he crossed you as well."

I turned to Palley, ignoring the man he claimed was his father. "I know this is very difficult for you. If you ever want to talk, you know where to find me."

"Can you stay a bit? I have some questions you might answer for me."

"Of course, Palley."

"Now, son, I'm sure Mrs. Reynolds has places to be," Mr. Haskell advised, giving me a frosty smile.

You know me. When a man puts my back up—I push back. I replied, "I'll wait, Palley. Take your time."

I didn't bother going up to the casket as it was closed, which told me the condition of Kathy's corpse. I shuddered at the thought of Palley discovering his mother in such a condition. Sitting in the back of the room, I watched people come and go—most of them disappointed the casket wasn't open. I sometimes think the human race are ghouls.

Detective Drake made an appearance, scanning the room. If Drake noticed me, he didn't show any sign. I'm sure he had an officer photographing visitors entering and leaving the funeral home, which told me the DA didn't think her case was ironclad, after all. Otherwise, why would he be here?

As I watched Palley greet visitors, I felt ashamed I could have entertained the notion he murdered his mother. He seemed like a shattered young man, deep in grief.

And I couldn't escape the notion that Dwight Haskell was watching me out of the corner of his eye.

The man gave me the creeps.

# 19

I sat in the back of the room, watching everyone until I felt a hand press upon my shoulder and squeeze. I looked up and around. Jumping Jehoshaphat! It was Agnes Bledsoe, my archenemy.

She leaned down, whispering, "Come with me, Josiah."

Like an obedient dog, I followed Agnes outside to her black Cadillac and got in.

"This will look awfully suspicious to the cop over there taking pictures," I claimed.

"We are old friends going for a cup of coffee," muttered Agnes, starting the car and driving away. She waved to the man taking snapshots of cars' license plates and drove several blocks away to a cemetery and parked.

I didn't make my usual digs or quips as Agnes looked distressed and not her usual cool, collected self. What's more unusual, she didn't verbally attack me either. Something was pressing on her mind.

After parking, she dug in her purse and pulled out a pack of cigarettes, lighting one.

"Are you kidding me? After having survived breast cancer?" I reached over to grab the ciggy, but Agnes slapped my hand away.

"Don't, Josiah. I smoke when agitated. I need this as it calms me."

"You and Lady Elsmere must form a club."

"Huh?"

"What do you want to discuss, Agnes? I've never seen you in such a state."

"I went to see Hunter. He's very depressed."

No. NO! I wasn't going to ask if he mentioned me. Instead, I remarked, "I'd think he would be."

Agnes inhaled deeply before blowing the smoke out the window. "Do you think he killed Kathy?"

"Everyone keeps asking that question."

"I think he might have."

Agnes' statement surprised me. "Why would you utter such a thing?"

"You remember me saying I used to babysit Hunter and Franklin when I was a teenager?"

"Yes, I remember."

"Their father gave me my first break in the horse business. That's when the family was flush with money and raised Thoroughbreds. I worked for the Wickliffes off and on until I was twenty-five, so I was around for a long time. I knew Kathy and Dwight Haskell as well."

"Come to the point, please." I wanted to get back to the funeral parlor as Palley might be searching for me.

"Hunter started dating Kathy in his sophomore year. She was a beautiful girl with a sparkling personality."

"I hear a *but* coming."

Agnes took another drag of her cigarette. "I didn't like her. Thought Kathy was rotten. I'm from eastern Kentucky, and Kathy was what we would refer to as sigogglin."

"What does that mean?"

"Something that is crooked or bent. I warned old man Wickliffe about the stories I had been hearing about Kathy, but he brushed them off, believing other teenage girls were jealous and spreading lies."

"What were the stories?"

"I'm not talking about stories of drinking, smoking, and carousing. We all raised a little hell when young. I'm talking about Kathy's character that ran deeper—darker."

"GET TO THE POINT, AGNES!"

"Kathy was Hunter's first love. He was over the moon about her. Hunter told me he was going to marry Kathy once he graduated college."

"What happened?"

"Hunter went off to college, and Kathy got a job in town. She began running around with Dwight Haskell and got pregnant, so they married. The marriage lasted for a few years until Dwight took a powder."

I counted the years. "It couldn't have been Palley. That's too far back. What happened to the child?"

"Kathy said she had a miscarriage, but I think she was never pregnant in the first place."

"Let me get the timeline right. Kathy married Dwight when she was nineteen?"

"Thereabouts. Hunter was finishing his freshman year of college."

"Okay. Then Dwight leaves town and Kathy files for a divorce."

"I guess Kathy filed for a divorce. Anyway, Dwight and Kathy are finished for the moment, but he comes back into the picture about ten years later."

"How so?"

"Kathy drifted to Florida and married her second husband."

"For how long?" I asked.

"About five years. This man was bad news. Sold drugs and only the Lord knows what else. He was killed during a drug drop, but Kathy was never charged or implicated in her husband's dealings."

I took a deep breath. This was a lot of information to take in. "This makes Kathy in her late twenties. When does Palley appear?"

"Kathy still came back frequently to see her parents. When in town, Kathy liked to hook up with old boyfriends. If Hunter was in town, she called him. If

Dwight drifted in to see his folks, she would do the same. This went on for years until she snagged John Sturgeon."

"She had Palley before she met Sturgeon."

"Yes, and her friends and family all agreed that Dwight was the father."

"But Dwight never remarried Kathy."

"I don't know why not. I only know Dwight never disputed publicly that Palley was his, so it was assumed by everyone he was the father. Even Dwight's kinfolk claimed Palley as their own."

"Just so I'm clear on this—both Hunter and Dwight were seeing Kathy when they were in town."

Agnes nodded. "Like dogs in heat. The pattern was broken when Hunter moved to Europe."

"How old is Palley when Kathy meets John Sturgeon?"

"About six. She met him at a medical conference in Tampa while working as a cocktail server. They married, and Sturgeon took them to California where he lived. They were together for about ten years before their marriage fell apart. Kathy came home when her father died a couple of years ago. She stayed as her mother fell ill and died soon after. Then guess what? She learns Hunter is back in the area as well and makes her move."

"Why would Kathy throw Hunter over for Dwight Haskell initially?"

"Dwight was quite the looker when young and could twirl a copperhead round his little finger if he had a mind to. Besides, both their natures were similar. Always one step ahead of the law."

"I knew Kathy had a sketchy past, but her arrest record shows bounced checks, speeding tickets, and shoplifting. Minor stuff."

"I've heard stories from my clients about Kathy being a blackmailer," Agnes announced.

That tidbit piqued my interest as Walter Neff had mentioned blackmail. "Who? A local person?"

Agnes nodded.

"How could Kathy know anything about anyone since she left town in her early twenties?"

"Her mother was a housekeeper, and her father worked for some of the famous horse farms in the area. Between the two of them, they supplied Kathy with plenty of information."

"For blackmail?"

"I think they thought they were gossiping with their daughter. I doubt they knew what she was up to."

"What was your friend's crime?"

"He doped his horses before a race."

"Why would this person confess such a thing to you?"

"He has retired, and it would be his word against mine if I filed a complaint, which I would never do. I would lose all my clients if I did that."

"Was it true?"

"Doesn't matter. Just a hint of doping will get a horse owner shunned by the racing community, even though many of them are guilty of the same infractions."

"How much did Kathy get from this guy?"

"Seventy-five thousand dollars over twenty years. She would call him and ask for money, saying she needed it for Palley. She posed the money as a loan, but it was really blackmail. It stands to reason Kathy had others on her speed dial. Why stop with one person?"

I whistled. "Seventy-five thousand is a substantial sum, but blackmail doesn't make sense, Agnes. Kathy was broke when she drifted into town. That's why Palley got a job with Hunter to save money for an old beater so he could win the prize money in the demolition derby."

"Wasn't telling Hunter that Palley was his son a kind of blackmail?"

"I guess you could say it might be, but Hunter welcomed it. He was extremely fond of Palley. If Kathy was blackmailing people, she didn't have to resort to marrying Hunter. He was financially stable, but not wealthy by any means."

Agnes shrugged. "I'm telling you there's more to the story of Hunter marrying Kathy than we know."

I didn't agree with Agnes, but let it slide. "When did your client tell you this story?"

"Last week when I took him to lunch."

I rolled down my window and waved away smoke. "This man spilled his guts over fried chicken?"

"It was shrimp salad if you must know. The subject of Kathy's death came up, and he blabbed the story. Seemed relieved to get it off his chest."

"When did Kathy last reach out to him?"

"Three weeks before she died."

"For how much?"

"I don't know. He said he refused, saying Hunter could pay for Palley now."

"Palley again. Well then. That's motive. This man could have killed Kathy. Did you tell Detective Drake?"

"I didn't have to tell him. Drake already knew about her past. Kathy was prosecuted for blackmail and extortion. She served two months in a Florida jail for blackmailing her boss. The man was skimming money from the hotel where they both worked. When he wouldn't pay her, Kathy ratted him out to the police. The boss got five years, and the hotel hired Kathy back when she was released."

I protested, "I never found any information about a prison term."

"You probably searched under the wrong married name. Kathy's had three husbands, not counting Hunter."

"Are any other former husbands in the Bluegrass

now besides Dwight Haskell?"

"Besides Dwight, there is John Sturgeon. He was at the visitation."

"Must be the out-of-state husband."

"California. He's a doctor, and Kathy's last husband before Hunter."

"What's his story with Kathy?" I inquired.

"I don't know, but I can't see Kathy shaking loose from a doctor's income. Maybe John Sturgeon divorced her."

I looked at my watch. "I need to get back, Agnes. Palley said he wanted to speak with me. I don't want to leave him in a lurch."

Agnes put her hand on my arm. "Look, Josiah. You're good at putting the pieces together. See what you can do for Hunter."

"I've been told by Hunter's lawyer to stay far away, and Hunter has not asked for my help."

Agnes pleaded again, "I don't think Hunter married Kathy because he loved her."

I took a deep breath. Talking about Hunter's reasons for marrying Kathy was painful. I had to admit the fact he dumped me wounded still. "Agnes, it doesn't matter why Hunter married the woman. He did marry her. I'm under no obligation to help him. You said yourself there was a possibility Hunter killed Kathy."

"I know, but I really don't believe it. Can't accept it as true of Hunter. Think about helping, Josiah."

Refusing to meet her eyes, I offered, "I'll not make any promises, but I will check into it."

"That's all I ask. Hunter's family was good to me, and I feel I owe him something."

We drove back to the funeral home in silence. I left my window wide open to disperse the rest of the cigarette smoke, but fingers of it lingered.

I couldn't wait to get out of Agnes' smoke-filled Cadillac.

# 20

I rushed into the receiving room, but I didn't see Palley near Kathy's coffin. I felt terrible about missing him. The crowd had thinned out, but I spied his father.

I approached Haskell deferentially as he seemed tense. "Hello, Mr. Haskell. Is Palley still here? I'd like to say goodbye before I leave."

"You were the girlfriend of Hunter Wickliffe," Haskell said.

It was a statement—not a question.

"Yes, Mr. Haskell. I've already told you when I met you earlier," I answered, wondering where Haskell was going with this.

"You're that detective lady always in the newspapers for solving murders."

"I'm not a detective, but I am good at looking at patterns of behavior."

"Why aren't you trying to solve Kathy's death?"

"Because whatever I would find, good or bad for Mr. Wickliffe, would be suspect and probably thrown out as evidence."

"It's a shame Hunter didn't murder you instead of Kathy."

Angry, I shot back, "Hunter didn't murder Kathy. However, you are a prime suspect in my book. You've been absent from Palley's life for years. I know you rarely paid child support. Now you've swooped back into the boy's life, acting like a savior. Why now? Did Kathy have a big life insurance policy?"

I was just throwing mud at the wall to see what stuck. However, Haskell's reaction frightened me. I thought he would deny my accusations quietly since we were in a public place. However, he stepped closer to me and smiled—a very creepy sneer, which unnerved me. I've seen this kind of smile before from the man who pulled me off a cliff, so I stepped back, knowing I had hit a nerve.

Haskell hissed, "You take care now. I'd hate to see a horse kick you in the head and have it caved in like Kathy."

Another visitor came up wishing to speak with Mr. Haskell, so I left quickly, realizing I had been threatened.

This put Mr. Haskell at the top of my list of suspects.

# 21

I never spoke to Palley. Unable to locate him at the funeral home, I texted, but received no reply. I left with a group of others departing while scanning the parking lot to see if Dwight Haskell followed. Because the man seemed dangerous, I needed to be careful. It was just something I felt.

Don't you get nasty vibes from people?

Driving home, I was both encouraged and cautious. I had a theory, but no facts to back it up. Needing more information, I texted Franklin.

Ten minutes later, he texted back saying he was at Wickliffe Manor for the night.

I asked if I could stop by as I was close. Not even waiting for an answer, I turned onto Old Frankfort Pike and hurried to the nineteenth-century Italianate-style brick villa listed on the National Register of Historic Places. The current home was built around an older domicile since the Wickliffes had been in Kentucky since the late 1700s. They had built their wealth from tobacco, hemp, and wheat crops worked by slave labor.

The luster of the Wickliffe name and wealth diminished bit by bit after the Civil War until Hunter inherited a run-down mansion and a farm steeped in debt. Now the current master of Wickliffe Manor was jailed for murder.

Maybe it was karma reaching out its sticky hand for past misdeeds of the family. Maybe it was kismet. Maybe Kathy's murder had nothing to do with the Wickliffe family history. Maybe it was just bad luck.

Remember my rule for murder. It was caused by sex, money, revenge, or a mix of all three. I knew Kathy had many enemies from her past, but why did the murder happen now? If what Agnes told me was true, why did Kathy resort to blackmailing again? Why were she and Hunter sleeping in different bedrooms? What did Palley want to tell me? Oh, I could kick myself for not being there for him.

The problem was I had more questions than answers. What did I know?

1.  Kathy was killed by blunt force trauma to the back of the head with a shovel or a manure rake at night. FACT.
2.  Kathy was murdered in the horse stable. FACT.
3.  If Agnes Bledsoe was to be believed, Kathy went to prison for blackmail and extortion. She

was still blackmailing people. HEARSAY.

4.  Walter mentioned Hunter had a DNA test done, stating he wasn't the father. FACT.

5.  Kathy might not have been legally divorced from her third husband when she married Hunter. HEARSAY.

6.  Hunter confessed to his wife's murder. FACT.

7.  Hunter then pleaded not guilty in court. FACT.

8.  Someone connected to Wickliffe Manor had rented rooms at the park lodge for assignations. FACT.

9.  Dwight Haskell was Palley's father. FACT.

10.  Hunter's and Kathy's marriage was in trouble. HEARSAY

That's all I knew. Everything else I gleaned was supposition. I needed facts—real concrete bits of truth. As I turned into the Wickliffe driveway, I hoped Franklin could supply some meaningful answers. I knew he had been dodgy with the truth.

# 22

Franklin, dressed in cut-off overalls with no shirt and flip-flops, waited on the portico as I arrived. "What's up?" he asked as I climbed the stairs to the red brick porch.

Puffing heavily, I fell into a white wicker chair. "Let me catch my breath."

Franklin brought over a tray of freshly made lemonade and ginger bars. He poured us both a glass and sat next to me. "You're out of shape if you can't climb these stairs."

Mumbling in a tired voice, I confessed, "I was over-stimulated at Kathy's visitation." Gratefully sipping the cold, invigorating lemonade, I fished the maraschino cherries out of the glass. After popping them in my mouth, I pressed the cool glass to my forehead.

"Tell me about it."

"Why weren't you there?" I asked Franklin.

"You think it appropriate for the brother of the man accused of murdering Kathy to attend her visitation. Put yourself in Palley's place. How would my appearance affect him?"

"Okay. Don't bite my head off. I'm not here about the visitation. I think you haven't been straight with me, Franklin. You know more than you're telling, and I want the truth, or I'm not doing another blessed thing to help Hunter."

He thrust the plate of ginger bars before me. "Have one. I made them myself."

"FRANKLIN!"

He put the plate down, but not before I snagged several, as I love ginger.

"The truth, Josiah, is that I don't know the actual story. Hunter will not confide in me. All I can tell you is I don't know why Hunter married Kathy. I don't know if Palley was the cause for the marriage. I don't know the rationale for Hunter's confession. I can only surmise from what I've witnessed, and I haven't spoken about my genuine thoughts as it might damage Hunter's case. I certainly don't want the district attorney to hear my concerns, and I don't want to testify against my big brother."

"Let's break this down into smaller parts. Anything you tell me is secondhand and would be thrown out in court if I was called to testify. Let's start with why you think Hunter married Kathy. The truth now. You're talking to me as you would under oath. No more half-baked truths or red herrings."

Franklin nodded, agreeing to tell the truth as it lay heavily on his conscience. "My belief is Kathy told Hunter that Palley was his son, and if he wanted access to him, Hunter had to marry Kathy. The deal was 'take care of us, and I will tell Palley you are his father to smooth the way for a relationship.'"

"Did Hunter know of Kathy's criminal past?"

His eyes widened. "I have no idea. What did she do?"

"Did you know Kathy went to prison for blackmail and extortion?"

Franklin shook his head, fluttering his hand across his face like a fan. "That's deep. I thought she was just a shallow, petty gold-digger who slept around. Didn't recognize she was so dark."

"Okay, now you went to the wedding."

"It was a paltry affair with family members from Kathy's side. It was Matt and me from the Wickliffe side."

"Do you remember Kathy's family?"

"Unfortunately yes. There was an ancient aunt and two first cousins with some second cousins trailing along. There was also a high school friend by the name of Amanda Prescott. She still lives in the area. The relatives live in the Cincinnati area."

"How was the wedding? Tell me the details."

"Kathy was beaming and telling everyone she got it right this time, because Hunter was her soul mate."

"Palley?"

"At the time everything seemed pleasant enough, but looking back at the reception, I noticed warning signs. Palley appeared upbeat, but I doubt he was ecstatic because of his mother's many past relationships. I would have to add Palley had great regard for Hunter. There was no alarm from Palley over Hunter. If the boy had any concerns, they would have had to do with his mother."

"Why do you say that?"

"Kathy was rowdy at the reception, bragging about snagging Hunter. I saw Palley whisper to her several times. He told the servers not to bring her any more champagne because Kathy embarrassed him."

"What was Hunter's demeanor?"

"He smiled a lot, mingled with the guests, stood patiently for the official wedding photos, showed affection to Kathy, and fox-trotted with the female guests at least once. In fact, he and Palley did a funny dance for Kathy. You know the type of dance I'm talking about—funny moves to song bites." Franklin thought back. "Yeah, it was a fun day, except for the fact Hunter was marrying Kathy."

"At what point did you notice the marriage going south?"

"It was several months after the wedding. I went to my old bedroom to get one of my childhood toys for Emmeline. To my surprise, Kathy's things were still in there—her clothes in the closet and her personal items in the bathroom. I went to the primary suite only to discover Hunter sleeping there. I assumed Palley was using the bedroom down the hall, but didn't have time to check as Hunter and Kathy came back into the house. They had been outside discussing reviving the formal garden."

"Anything else?"

"I saw less and less of Hunter, and when I did, he was quiet. When I asked about Kathy, he replied she was fine. If I asked about Palley, Hunter would gush about what a neat kid he was. Hunter's face would light up."

"I've asked you before, but do you believe Palley is Hunter's son?"

"I doubt it. I knew Hunter hooked up with Kathy when she came back to visit her parents, but those two look nothing alike as father and son. And Palley didn't favor Kathy either, except for blue eyes."

I reminded him, "Kathy and Palley both had blond hair."

Franklin held up a finger. "Bottle blond there. Her actual hair color was brown. Kathy started dyeing it in her freshman year. I know because I taught her how."

"Any other alarm bells?"

"Hunter called Matt wanting to discuss financial matters. I thought it odd as Matt does Hunter's taxes, but he is not a financial advisor. He is a tax lawyer."

"Go on."

"After Matt met with Hunter, I asked about it. Matt said he couldn't tell me about the meeting due to lawyer-client privilege. I made the comment 'that serious, huh,' and Matt said it was."

"I suspect all sorts of scenarios went through your mind."

"They did."

"What's the status of Hunter's bank records?"

"Hunter went paperless, so I couldn't find any bank records that way. The police took all the computers, including Palley's."

"Don't you have access to those records, Franklin, since your name is on the farm's deed? You can go to the bank and request paper copies for the past year."

"I told Hunter not to add my name to any financial records, as I have a problem with our family's history of using enslaved people. I didn't want to be involved in restoring the farm. But Hunter refused to sell the land and kept my name on the deed. Now I'm saddled with this headache. If Hunter goes to prison, I'm getting rid of the farm."

"Franklin, if we took on the guilt for the harm our ancestors did, we'd never get out of bed. Let the past be the past."

My friend twisted his mouth, giving one of those *you-don't-understand* looks.

I changed the subject. "Speaking of the farm, I

thought you were going to ask the Dupuy boys to help?"

"Malcolm arrives tomorrow morning, with his older brother coming in the afternoon. I'm bugging out for home then."

It was getting dark, and I wanted to get going. I disliked driving at night anymore. Another sign of aging. "If you think of anything else, call me. I'm piecing things together, but there are big gaps of information missing."

Franklin offered more cookies, trying to stall me from leaving. Being alone at Wickliffe Manor was not something he enjoyed. "What happened at the visitation?"

"I met Palley's biological father."

Franklin's eyes widened. "For real?"

"I don't think I'm mistaken about it. They looked like doppelgangers."

"Dwight Haskell? It's been long said Dwight was the boy's father."

"Palley introduced him as such at the visitation."

"How did Dwight act?"

"I think he threatened me."

"You don't know?"

"He said he wished Hunter had murdered me instead, and I should watch out for horses kicking me in the head."

"Dwight was always a bully in high school—a big

jerk. Hunter had to fight him all the time. Someone like me made a perfect target for Dwight's anger, and Hunter would stand up for me."

"Who won?"

"Dwight was taller and had thirty pounds of pure muscle on Hunter, but my big brother held his own. I would say Hunter gave as good as he got."

I don't know why, but that pleased me. Pleased me very much.

# 23

I was unlocking my front door when the landline phone rang. It was Matt. Tired and thirsty, I was reluctant to answer it, but it could be important since I had just come from Wickliffe Manor. "Hello?"

"Franklin says you weaseled out Hunter's call to me."

"Can't you say hello first before you chastise me?"

"Jo, I've been subpoenaed to testify at the preliminary hearing."

"About this meeting between you and Hunter?"

"I'm sure the police learned what I discovered."

"How would they know about the two of you working on an audit?"

"From Hunter's computer. I had to use it to go through his books."

"I just walked through the door, Matt. Let me put my purse down before you say anything further. Hold on."

I threw my purse onto a side table and kicked off

my pumps. The patio light was on, and Baby and the Kitty Kaboodle were pawing at the back door wanting to come in for the night. I almost laughed. You'd think they were stranded on the side of the road with no food or water in the blazing sun. They looked so pitiful, but they would have to wait.

"Okay, I'm back."

"I want you to know this before I testify. If the DA skips the preliminary hearing and takes this to a grand jury, my testimony will be sealed until I'm called to the murder trial."

"I'm listening."

"Hunter called a month before Kathy died. He was missing money and wanted me to check his accounting books."

"You're not a CPA."

"I recommended one from my firm, but Hunter said he wanted to keep this within the family. He wouldn't tell me what he suspected. Said he needed a thorough going through of all his bank accounts and asked me to keep it between the two of us. I obliged."

"What did you find out?"

"It was a daunting task, but it seemed the accounts for the farm had been cooked. I checked invoices against incoming and outgoing checks and bank transfers, finding they didn't match. Not all incoming payments for horse boarding were listed, and last fall's tobacco and soybean sales were not recorded properly.

Hunter kept every invoice and receipt, so I went through boxes of paper to compare against the computer spreadsheets. Now Hunter's personal accounts were fine. It was only the accounts for the farm that were in disarray."

"The upshot?"

"Fifteen thousand dollars was missing, give or take a little change. I gave the information to Hunter."

"And?"

"He directed me again not to say anything to Franklin."

"When did you tell Franklin?"

"When I got the subpoena. I said Hunter had me look at discrepancies in his accounts—nothing more. I would prefer you didn't tell Franklin that I called. Please keep this information to yourself for now. It would freak Franklin out. I would rather he hears it at the hearing. The DA will have her own CPA testify."

"What a mess, Matt."

"So far I've been able to hide behind lawyer-client privilege dodging the police, but that will end with the hearing."

"What's your take on the matter?"

"I went back eighteen months. Everything was in sync until three months after Hunter married Kathy."

"Oh boy, this is not going to look good for Hunter."

"I have to tell the truth, Josiah. I'll be under oath.

As much as I like and respect Hunter, I'm not going to jail for perjury."

"Agreed, Matt. Tell the truth. It's all you can do."

"Thanks, Jo. Your saying so means a lot to me. Look, I've got to go. I'll talk to you later." Matt hung up.

Another nail in Hunter's coffin.

If the police could prove Kathy was having an affair plus embezzling and determined Hunter knew—it would be a slam dunk for the man's conviction.

It had to be Kathy stealing. I certainly didn't think Palley was robbing Hunter.

Two good motives for murder.

Men have killed their wives for less.

# 24

Baby thumped his tail against the wall to wake me up.

"Stop it, Baby!" I grumbled.

When that didn't work, the mastiff came over to the bed and jiggled the mattress with his massive head, whimpering.

Then I heard a kitty jump onto my dresser and knock items to the floor.

Jumping Jehoshaphat! Would these freaking animals give me no peace?

Flinging the covers back, I leaped out of bed, yelling.

The Kitty Kaboodle ran into the living room, happy they had successfully gotten their human out of bed.

Baby stayed and watched as I tinkled, brushed my teeth, and washed my face. I have no idea why dogs find humans performing their ablutions so fascinating.

Grumpy and still not fully awake, I put the cats and Baby outside on the pool patio where I fed them. Once they filled their bellies, the cats scampered off to play, while I struggled to clean the folds on Baby's face.

When he growled, I tapped him hard on the noggin. "That's no way to talk to me. Be good. You can't go out in public looking like this."

He pulled his massive head away in contempt, but I had a secret weapon. I reached for the oatmeal treat I had stashed in my pocket. Acting as though I was munching it, Baby swung his head around. He sniffed the air and thumped his tail on the ground.

"I have a treat for you, but only if you are a good boy. Cooperate and you may get it." I waved the oatmeal treat under his nose and quickly stored it in my back pocket.

Baby whined, watching it disappear.

I held out the washcloth. "Ready?"

Baby complied and stopped fussing, finally getting his reward. I didn't even witness him chewing it, as he inhaled the treat.

All mastiffs have similar temperaments. They are an ancient breed. Julius Caesar brought them from Britain for the Roman circuses. They accompanied knights on the Crusades and were destroyed if the knight fell in battle because nobody could approach the body otherwise. Mostly, they were trained to lie in the master's castle doorway as they were exceptional guards. During WWII, the breed almost died out. English breeders sent mating pairs and beloved pets to

Canadian volunteers when the British government asked the population to euthanize their pets, if the owner felt he or she could not evacuate the animals when the Germans attacked. Ships loaded with panting, willful, and frightened brindle, fawn, and apricot-colored mastiffs crossed the pond to safety.

Baby is a fawn descendant of the WWII Canadian Mastiffs. He is willful, lazy, and massive, but I love him, and he returns my affection. Baby is my buddy, and I am his.

I can't express why I am so close to this animal.

I just am.

I'm glad Baby woke me up because the alarm didn't go off. Perhaps I forgot to set it. Anyway, I had a funeral to attend, and I was going to be late.

# 25

I got to the cemetery as they offloaded the casket from the hearse. Walking behind a group of mourners, I gaped at everyone attending. The group was small, allowing me to recognize several people from the visitation the day before. I made a mental note of everyone, hoping my memory would hold up—Palley, Dwight Haskell, Kathy's ancient aunt and the two cousins, a tall brunette with an hourglass figure wearing a fascinator with a veil, and a distinguished-looking man with a military haircut in an expensive tailored suit.

A man whispered, "Pathetically small group of mourners for a woman who's lived for some fifty-odd years on this earth."

Looking behind me, I spied Eli Bradley lounging against a tree. "Stop that," I scolded. "Disrespectful."

Bradley moved beside me, removing his hat as the group bowed their heads to pray.

"Why are you here?" I hissed, watching the crowd. I noticed the woman with the veiled fascinator didn't bow her head as everyone else did.

"Best way to see all the principal players. Anyone look guilty to you?"

"Everyone looks guilty to me."

"Palley doesn't. He looks absolutely grief-stricken."

We both glanced over at Palley, who had tears streaming down his face. Dwight Haskell took a handkerchief from his breast pocket and handed it to the boy. Putting his arm around Palley, he pulled the grieving boy close.

"At least Haskell is acting like a father."

"Thought you might want to know you were right. Dwight Haskell is Palley's biological father. The DA sent over the new DNA results. There's a motive for killing Kathy right there."

The minister shot the two of us a dirty look before saying, "Amen."

Everyone raised their heads, including Bradley and myself.

"Who's the statuesque brunette with the veil?"

"I think it is Kathy's high school girlfriend—Amanda Prescott. The tall man with the military bearing and haircut must be Kathy's third husband—John Sturgeon. He fits the description I was given."

"Gossip?"

"Yep. Fresh off the vine."

"What does he do, Mrs. Reynolds?"

"He's some kind of doctor. A surgeon, perhaps? I

don't remember."

"Hmm."

"Why are you really here, Mr. Bradley?"

"Like I mentioned—putting names to faces and seeing how people interact with each other. I have a man taking pictures with a telescopic lens and another taking down the license plate numbers of the mourners' cars."

"Looks like you have everything covered."

Bradley turned to me. "I need to speak with you again. A few things have come up, which I need clarified."

"Not here. Not now. Come to the Butterfly after five. That's all the time I can spare." I moved away from Bradley and stood by myself. Out of the corner of my eye, I saw Bradley speaking with a man holding a camera and then leaving. Turning my attention to a soloist, I listened to her singing *Wayfaring Stranger* a cappella.

> I'm just a poor wayfaring stranger
> Traveling through this world below
> There is no sickness, no toil, no danger
> In that bright land to which I go
> I'm going there to see my father
> And all my loved ones who've gone on
> I'm just going over Jordan
> I'm just going over home

I know dark clouds will gather 'round me
I know my way is hard and steep
But beauteous fields arise before me
Where God's redeemed, their vigils keep
I'm going there to see my mother
She said she'd meet me when I come
So I'm just going over Jordan
I'm just going over home I'm just going over Jordan
I'm just going over home

While the songstress' mournful rendition deeply touched me, it completely unhinged Palley, who flung himself against his mother's coffin positioned on a bier above the gravesite.

There was a loud cry of dismay as we watched the coffin wobble while men rushed to stabilize it. They were not quick enough to grasp the coffin, which fell upside down, catching itself between the earth and the metal bier meant to underpin it. The top popped open, allowing an arm to tumble out.

Dwight Haskell dragged Palley to his car and quickly drove away while Palley screamed.

"My God!" I moaned under my breath.

A hushed silence hung in the air among the attendees until the minister beckoned us all to leave. "There's no more to see here, folks. Let these men put Katherine Wickliffe to right."

It took more encouragement for others to leave as

they seemed stunned at Palley's actions. The minister went to the man I surmised was John Sturgeon and talked with him for several minutes. Seeing he was getting nowhere with Sturgeon refusing to leave, I walked up to them.

"Excuse me, gentlemen. I'm quite shaken. Could one of you escort me to my vehicle?"

The minister glanced at Sturgeon. "Could you, sir? I want to be with Kathy until she's in the ground. Her family belonged to my church, and I baptized her. I wish to pray over her as she descends to her last earthly home."

I quickly agreed, "I'm sure she would appreciate that, Pastor." Looking hopefully at Sturgeon, I asked, extending my arm, "Sir?"

Perturbed, but resigned, Sturgeon encircled my arm with his.

"My name is Josiah Reynolds. Who might you be?"

"Were you a friend of Kathy's?" he asked, ignoring my question.

"Not exactly. I was Hunter Wickliffe's particular friend before his marriage to Kathy."

Sturgeon stopped and unwrapped my arm. Gazing intently at me, he replied, "That's interesting. I am Kathy's husband. I was, I mean."

"You mean her third husband."

"I never divorced Kathy. Her marriage to Hunter Wickliffe was illegal. I can prove it."

"That's interesting."

"I suppose you are here to dig something up to get your former boyfriend off the hook. I hate to tell you that my still being married to Kathy gives Wickliffe a motive."

"I don't see why. He could have just walked away from her, but you, on the other hand, are a suspect in my book."

Sturgeon reached over and squeezed my arm. "What do you think you have on me?"

I pulled away. "Hey, that hurts, buddy."

Sturgeon grabbed me again and squeezed harder. I looked around for help, but no one was looking our way. "Why are you here, lady?"

I jerked my bruised arm away from the man. "It's at times like this I wish I carried a pistol. I can see why Kathy left you."

Sturgeon pushed me. That's right. HE PUSHED ME! Why was this man so hostile?

"Is there a problem here?"

We both turned to see the minister standing a few feet away from us with a disapproving expression on his face. I could tell the minister didn't like John Sturgeon, but wasn't thrilled about me either. I immediately jumped at the opportunity to extract myself from John Sturgeon. "Yes, Pastor. My van is right over there. Might you help me?"

"Of course." The minister put his arm around my

waist, escorting me to my van. I thanked him profusely while climbing into the vehicle. I couldn't wait to get out of there, but not trusting John Sturgeon, I hid the van behind a mausoleum. After seeing him drive out of the cemetery, I gave Sturgeon a ten-minute start.

I never wanted to be alone with Kathy's third husband again. He was a nutcase, who had no impulse control and a short fuse. If he acted like that with a stranger, what might he do to his family?

Kathy's reason for leaving California was obvious.

My guess is she fled in fear.

# 26

"Thank you for seeing me again," Mr. Bradley said.

"Can you tell me what this is about? I've had a hard day, and I would like to get this interview over as soon as possible."

Bradley raised an eyebrow. "What happened to gracious Southern hospitality?"

"It died at the cemetery today."

"Yes, I heard about the debacle. I had a man film it. You also had a run-in with John Sturgeon."

I held out my arm and displayed my bruises. "Look at this. I'm lucky the cretin didn't rip my arm off. What's that guy's story, anyway?"

Bradley paused for a moment. "I'm going to trust you, Mrs. Reynolds, to keep your mouth closed. I can see you are trying to help Mr. Wickliffe."

Shaking my head, I avowed, "Not my circus. Not my monkeys."

Bradley gave a wisp of a smile. "I think the lady doth protest too much."

Noticing Bradley had cute dimples when he smiled, I said, "I'm curious about this visit—that's all."

"Let's play tit for tat. I'll tell you what I know, and you tell me what you know."

I invited, "You go first."

"I did some digging on Mr. Sturgeon. There were several police calls to his house. Palley made the calls."

"I figured it was something like that. Kathy had the worst taste in men—Haskell abandoned her and their son, second husband was a drug runner, and John Sturgeon—allegedly a wife-beater."

"She had little luck with men, that's for sure. Kathy Wickliffe liked *bad boys*."

"What else did you find out about John Sturgeon?"

Bradley said, "He may have hit Kathy, but he has a clean record as a doctor, and from all accounts, he is beloved by his staff and patients. Doesn't drink, gamble, or chase women. Pays his bills on time and has a fat bank account."

"What about former girlfriends?" I inquired.

"My man is currently contacting them. Here's something interesting, though. I have a buddy with the Louisville police who ran a trace on Sturgeon's phone."

"Isn't that illegal?"

Ignoring my question, Bradley said, "It pinged near Wickliffe Manor several days before Kathy died."

"What was Sturgeon doing in Kentucky?" I wondered aloud.

"Now you're gonna love this. Sturgeon had a life insurance policy on Kathy for five-hundred-thousand."

"Who's the beneficiary?"

"Sturgeon," Bradley answered.

"Is he in financial trouble?"

"Not that I can find."

"Has he made a claim?"

"Not yet."

"Anyone else have an insurance policy on Kathy?"

"Hunter had a small policy on Kathy, but a larger one on himself with Palley being the beneficiary."

"Hey, things are looking up. All you have to do is suggest Sturgeon as a possible suspect. Create reasonable doubt."

"I am considering this strategy. With the film I have of Sturgeon grabbing and pushing you, I think I can make an excellent case of homicidal rage occurring when Kathy left him. There's one problem."

"What is it?"

"Even if the jury finds Hunter Wickliffe not guilty, it doesn't prove his innocence in the public's mind. His career would still be ruined, as there is the matter of the confession."

"Has Hunter explained the confession?"

"Nope. He's one of the worst clients I've ever had. He does little for his own defense."

"Can't help you there."

"You have no idea why Mr. Wickliffe is so reticent?"

"I first thought it had to do with Palley. Maybe Hunter is trying to protect the boy, but after seeing the film of Palley falling apart at the cemetery, I reject such an idea. You can't fake such deep grief."

"I think the opposite. It was too over the top. My theory is Palley meant to desecrate his mother's burial using sorrow as a cover."

Horrified, I contested, "Surely not. There was heart-felt grief expressed, but the casket tipping over was a terrible accident."

Bradley shot a dubious look toward me. "The woman's casket upended with the top springing open, and the dead woman almost plunged face down into her own grave. I think that's a little extreme. Palley put real force into flinging himself onto the coffin. I don't think it was an accident."

I didn't know how to respond. Eli Bradley's theory about Palley was repugnant.

Matricide?

Jumping Jehoshaphat!

# 27

Baby pawed at the back window. He scratched the glass, making a sound like the screech of chalk on an old-fashioned blackboard, which those of us who have been around a while know.

"Why don't we take a break?" Bradley suggested.

"We're not finished?"

"Not by a long shot."

"Get outta of town."

Bradley gave a puzzled look.

I responded, "Get out of town as in—surely you jest?"

"No, really. I have more to discuss with you, but first, I would like to meet Baby." Bradley craned his neck to look at the dog through the glass. "What's that sitting on his head?"

"One of Baby's pet cats." I rose and opened the patio door, letting in a rambunctious mastiff and five scampering barn cats. They rushed to greet the unfamiliar human. The animals were quite rude, sniffing Mr.

Bradley and pulling at his pant legs.

I had to shoo them away. "I'm so sorry. They get excited when they see someone new."

Bradley chuckled. "Don't be. I love animals, but have no pets because of my work. I confess I came early so I could walk about your farm and visit the animals. I lost count of the number of species you house. This farm is sort of a sanctuary, isn't it?"

Feeling friendlier toward Mr. Bradley, I inquired, "You saw only the domesticated animals. There is much diversity with the wildlife, too."

"Really?"

"There are groundhogs, chipmunks, squirrels, possums, skunks, weasels, otters, foxes, owls, hawks, deer, coyotes, and bobcats as well. Lady Elsmere and I have planted fruit/nut-bearing trees/shrubbery as well as native seed-bearing plants for the animals at the back of the farm."

"How do you protect your domesticated animals from the predators?"

"Simple—donkeys."

"Donkeys?"

"They run off the predators and keep the other animals in line as well. Of course, the horses return to the stable by dusk."

"Donkeys! Who would have *thunk* it, eh?"

I was getting to like Mr. Bradley more and more. "Would you like a slice of rhubarb pie? Wash it down with cold milk or a shot of bourbon? I have both.”

“Did you make the pie? From scratch?”

“Good sir, you cut me to the quick,” I teased.

“By all means. The rumor is that you are a fine cook.”

“I’m passable, but Miss Bess, at the Big House, is considered the best chef in the Bluegrass.”

“The Big House refers to Lady Elsmere’s domicile. Correct? I’m trying to place all these big estates in my mind.”

“Correct.”

Mr. Bradley had several cats on his lap while another one lay contentedly on his yellow legal pad. Jealous, Baby took his nose and rooted the two cats from their comfortable perch so he could lay his head directly on Mr. Bradley’s knees, peering up at him with those sad brown eyes of his.

I didn’t force the animals away this time. Bradley had assured that he wanted to see the animals. *Well, Mr. Bradley, I hope the cats don’t shed too much hair on your expensive suit, and Baby doesn’t leave a ribbon of glistening slime on your pants.*

I smiled, cutting the rhubarb pie and pouring the milk. I knew Bradley was after something, though I wasn’t sure what, and yeah, I can be petty.

“Let me help you.”

Startled, I jumped, turning around with the pie knife.

"I'm sorry. I thought you heard me. Didn't mean to surprise you," Bradley said, picking up the plates of pie.

I followed Mr. Bradley back into the great room with the milk. He sat at the Nakashima table facing the back windows. I sat beside him, watching him watch the birds at the feeders as we ate in silence.

"Another piece?" I asked after he had wolfed his down.

"No, thank you. The pie was delicious. I have to confess it was my first time eating rhubarb. Tasted like strawberries."

"That's because strawberries are mixed in with the rhubarb."

"Do you run this farm all by yourself?"

"Oh, goodness, no. I have hired help. Mostly Charles Dupuy's grandsons help with the animals. If I need more assistance, I call friends. I tend the bees and mow fields."

"Mr. Dupuy used to be Lady Elsmere's butler."

"He's now her estate manager and heir. When she passes, everything will go to Charles' family. His grandsons are being trained to run the estate as Charles is not a young man himself."

"I understand you brokered this amazing bit of fortune for the Dupuys."

"I merely helped Lady Elsmere come to a decision she would have made, eventually. Charles is an honorable man, and his family helped build this country."

"Yes, I understand his ancestors worked for Henry Clay, and a Charlotte Dupuy sued the Great Compromiser for her freedom."

"Yes, you know what burns my britches? Charlotte Dupuy, one of the first enslaved women to sue a powerful man like Henry Clay for freedom, doesn't have one stinking statue or even a plaque in this town. Do you know how much guts it took for Charlotte to take on Henry Clay? This family should take their place among the elites of this town. It's only fitting."

"I know you are especially close to Lady Elsmere. Why didn't you connive to have her leave you the money?"

I drew back. "It never occurred to me, besides she gave me a million dollars plus jewelry she wanted me to have. With my settlement from the city concerning my accident and my pension when I hit sixty-five, I have enough to take care of my needs. My daughter will inherit the farm."

"Farms."

"Excuse me."

"You took the million dollars Lady Elsmere gave you and purchased the farm next door. You are the owner of two farms."

"Are you hinting at something?" I didn't like Bradley prying into my private affairs.

"I find it interesting that a woman with such resources boards horses, has a catering business, rents her house out for events, and trots down to the farmers' market to sell honey every Saturday."

"I wasn't always this flush. There was a time after my husband passed away I came near to losing the Butterfly. This house means the world to me."

"Do you think it's time to slow down?"

"That time will come sooner rather than later. Why are you so interested?"

"I'm interested in you, Mrs. Reynolds." Mr. Bradley locked eyes with me and didn't waver.

I hadn't had this type of intimacy in a long time. Quite frankly, it unnerved me. I looked away, but not before my heart raced. I knew my face was blushing.

If Mr. Bradley was embarrassed, he didn't show it, but seemed amused at my discomfort.

"Is there anything else you wish to discuss with me before you leave, Mr. Bradley?"

"I see I have my marching orders, but yes, I do. I want to talk about Mr. Wickliffe."

"What about Hunter?"

"Mr. Wickliffe is finally out on bail. He wears a leg bracelet and must stay put at Wickliffe Manor unless it is to visit the courts, the police, a doctor, or his lawyer."

"That's wonderful news. I worried Hunter would be attacked in jail."

"Is it wonderful?"

"Well, yes. I think Hunter to be an innocent man."

"That is why I wish you to see Mr. Wickliffe and

speak with him."

"No, I'm not going to see Hunter. We are done," I replied, shaking my head emphatically.

"I don't think you are *done* with Hunter Wickliffe, Mrs. Reynolds, and you may be the one person to draw him out. I need to know what is motivating his actions and what he knows. He will not trust me. This man must tell me everything so I can fight for him."

I didn't know how to respond. "Hunter has not asked to see me. I will not invade his privacy. It would look like—look like—." I couldn't finish the sentence.

"Like you're throwing yourself at him?"

"That's it. Exactly," I answered, snapping my fingers.

"Mrs. Reynolds, please. You once loved this man. Won't you help me save him?"

Darn it! What could I say?

# 28

I had to get my honey to the fair.

It takes two hours to reach the Kentucky State Fair in Louisville. My glass jars of honey were carefully swathed in bubble wrap and stashed in the back of the Buick borrowed from Lady Elsmere. This was a big, old vintage car the size of an aircraft carrier. It had belonged to her first husband, and June refused to part with it. Driving it was like driving a tank, so I knew my jars would be safe. I had two jars each of Black Locust honey, Clover honey, and Wildflower honey carefully positioned in a cardboard box on the floor of the back seat.

Every time hitting a bump I froze, even though I knew my jars were safe. The fear that one of my jars would suffer damage was irrational, but overwhelming. That's why I always brought two jars. Glass jars have shattered en route to the fair or been dropped by an anxious beekeeper when entering the judging area.

And then there were the occasional hijinks by a

competing beekeeper. My stress level was on a high note until the beekeeping staff accepted, tagged, and locked my jars in the display case.

I also brought two frames of capped honey.

These frames were judged on how completely the honeybees covered the frame with beeswax plus the color, evenness, and neatness of the wax on the frame. It was basically a judgment on the bees themselves. A frame leaking honey was automatically disqualified.

Parking in a handicapped parking space, I put my frames and jars in a portable wagon I brought and made my way into the honey pavilion. I carefully pulled my two frames out of their containers and placed them in the display case allowing a volunteer beekeeper to tag the wooden top of the frame with location of the hive. After securing the frames, she handed me the bottom of the identification-numbered ticket. Names were not allowed until after the judging, thus the need for a numbered tag, which I would guard jealously until the judges had made their rounds.

Let's talk about beeswax. Honeybees are born with beeswax plugs on their abdomen, which they pull out and chew, making the plugs malleable. Pretty neat, huh!

In olden times, bees were kept not only for the honey, but also for the wax. Beeswax candles were paid to the state and to the church in lieu of taxes and tithes because the candles smelled sweet when lit. They were very sought after, and only the rich could afford them.

Even today, beeswax candles are expensive. I give them away as gifts and sell the candles at the farmers' market.

Beeswax is still applicable for furniture making, medicine, cosmetics, sewing, and numerous other uses. The wax is collected after the honey is uncapped and strained. Those beekeepers, who don't make candles, sell the beeswax to beekeeping firms, which clean and resell it.

But I digress. After my frames and honey jars were safely ensconced in their respective display cases, I gossiped with beekeepers from other parts of Kentucky. Everyone was having trouble with mites, pesky invasive insects from Asia. They were all angry about cheap honey, infused with corn syrup, sold in grocery stores as pure honey. After an hour of tongue-wagging with my fellow beekeepers, I visited the rest of the fair before heading home.

I wandered through the vegetable display room and watched two men bring in the largest pumpkin I had ever seen on a forklift. It must have weighed over a thousand pounds. It was a struggle, but they shifted the pumpkin onto a specialized padded platform without creating any cracks on its surface. I mentally calculated the number of pies that could be made from that one pumpkin—maybe eight hundred or more.

Next, I hit the livestock area. Teenagers and children as young as nine were leading their fifteen-hundred pound milk cows into their stalls. Their parents followed, hauling bedding, chairs, ice chests, and extra clothes for the kids.

The dairy cows contentedly munched on hay left out for them as their water, food, and straw beds had been prepared beforehand. I asked one young lady if I could pet her Holstein as she brushed the gentle black and white giant.

"Sure, but step where she can see you or she might kick if startled."

"Gonna get the blue ribbon this year?" I chatted while stroking the soft jaw of the munching cow.

"You bet. I bottle-fed this cow since a calf. She's very friendly and loves attention."

"I can see that. What's her name?"

"Janet."

"Janet? Is she named after someone?"

"No, I just like the name Janet."

"What's your name?"

"Millie."

"Nice to meet you, Millie. My name is Mrs. Reynolds. Thank you for letting me pet Janet."

"Sure thing."

Meandering among the Jerseys, I stopped to watch a young man shampoo his dairy cow. A family of four watched also, and their little boy asked if the brown cow made chocolate milk.

The young handler explained that all cows' milk was white, prompting chuckles from the adults. The teenager stated an exhibition was happening two aisles away if the family wanted to see a cow milked. Excited, they rushed to see the milking, while I dashed to the parking lot. I had spent more time than intended and needed to get home.

I took the expressway until Frankfort and got off to drive on the back roads. It would be another forty-five minutes before I walked into the Butterfly where a furious Baby awaited me. I knew he'd be annoyed at being alone for hours, particularly when smelling other animals on me. The evening was going to be uncomfortable with Baby ignoring me. That's how he punished me. I would deal with him later. Right now I had to concentrate on the road.

Kentucky back roads are curvy and narrow. One had to be careful when navigating them. Old timers drive in the middle of the road and move over into their lane when they see another car heading toward them. That works okay except around a curve. City drivers out for an afternoon country excursion drive too fast, underestimating the hairpin curves and loose farm animals standing in the middle of the road.

The borrowed Buick handled the roads better than my 1960s VW van could, so I was happy—until the rain started. First, it drizzled with the sun shining, then the heavens opened up. Southerners refer to this type of rain as *Satan beating his wife*. I don't know who would marry the devil, but there it is.

Dark gray clouds filled the sky, and the wind grew, causing the trees to sway.

The rain was too heavy for the windshield wipers, so I needed to pull over—but where?

What fresh hell was this? Something moved on the road. I slowed to a crawl. It moved again, heading straight for the car. What was it? Fortunately, I was on a stretch of straight road, so I stopped the car and flicked on the emergency blinkers. Whatever it was, it ran to the driver's side of the car. Upon rolling down the window, I heard scratching and whimpering at the door.

Jumping Jehoshaphat! It was a dog. A puppy, in fact! I opened the door and pulled the drenched animal in and put it on the back seat.

Seeing its emaciated condition, I recognized it must have been chucked. Thinking there might be more puppies, I got out of the car and searched among the weeds near the road. I discovered three more puppies concealed in the briars by the side of the road. After much begging and cursing, I pulled them from their hiding place and put them in the car. I searched for another ten minutes. No more puppies.

Soaked and bleeding from the briar thorns, I rushed to my vet's office fifteen minutes away. Luckily, her office was open as I drove into the parking lot. Gathering four frightened, wiggling puppies was not a simple task, but I did it and even pulled the door open to get into the dry office.

Since the puppies and I were dripping water on the floor, a clerk promptly led us to an exam room, providing towels. I was a mess and probably looked as miserable as the soaked canines. I dried myself as best I could and then turned my attention to the puppies. They were shivering, and two piddled on the floor.

The ungrateful puppies growled as I tried to dry them off. One even nipped me. "I should have left you on the road, you little turd," I barked.

"What have we got here, Josiah?" asked the vet as she walked into the room. This was my new vet after my old one, George, tried to kill me last winter.

Immediately, the four puppies huddled in a corner, hiding their faces.

"A bunch of ungrateful whelps. I found them stranded near Keene on Route 169."

"Why are you bleeding?"

"I had to pull three of them out from a briar patch," I confessed heatedly.

The vet chuckled, said, "No good deed goes unpunished."

"With my luck, they probably have rabies. One bit me."

Amused, the vet recommended, "Wash up at the sink while I examine these vicious animals. There's an antiseptic cream on the shelf above."

I made a face as I squinted and wrinkled my nose. "Ha-ha, Masie."

Masie picked one puppy up and placed it on a table. She took its temperature, checked his mouth and ears, listened to his heart, and probed with her fingers. One by one, she checked the shivering puppies. "Well, Josiah, I've got some good news and some bad news."

"Oh dear, how much is this going to cost me?"

"I can treat them here, or you can take them to the pound where they will treat them for free."

I hesitated. "I don't know about taking them to the pound. They're awfully young."

"About seven weeks. They are in relatively good health considering they are undernourished. They are covered in fleas and in need of a bath. Right now, we need to get them warm and fed. If you give me a moment, I will have my techs wrap them up in warm blankets and give them something to eat. I'll even loan you a laundry basket to carry them home."

"A laundry basket?"

"They are cheap and great for transporting young kittens and puppies. Don't worry. I'm only going to charge you what is cost me for the basket."

"They need their shots, Masie."

"I will also give them deworming medication as well. Now leave, please, and go to the front desk to pay the bill while my staff takes care of these little critters."

I did what I was told. Forty-five minutes and five-hundred dollars and a few cents later, I walked out with four sleepy puppies, medicine, plus four bags and twelve cans of special dog food.

Fortunately, it had stopped raining.

Masie walked out with me, carrying the dog food. "Bring them back in two weeks."

"I've already made the appointment, you robber baron. You can thank me for fronting your next month's mortgage payment on your fancy new office. Geez, five-hundred dollars."

"You've got some special dogs there, Jo. They will need to be trained if you're going to keep them."

I looked down at the basket of puppies. "What? These mutts?"

Masie put the dog food in the trunk. "These mutts are actually prized purebreds."

Surprised, I asked, "What are they?"

"Pure Mountain Curs. They are the breed Daniel Boone and other pioneers brought with them through the Cumberland Gap into Kentucky. They are very rare. Take good care of them. They are worth a great deal of money."

I couldn't fathom some thoughtless person dumping four helpless puppies in the middle of nowhere—much less—expensive puppies. Didn't make sense to me, but I remembered people can often be stupid and heartless when dealing with animals. Then I recalled my two-hundred pound mastiff at home.

Lord Almighty! How would Baby react to these squirming bundles of fur?

# 29

I parked Lady Elsmere's boat-sized Buick in front of the Butterfly's double doors and looked in the rearview mirror at the basketful of puppies. They had been lulled to sleep by the motion of the car, but suddenly came to life when it stopped. Two of them stretched onto their hind legs and peered over the handle of the basket.

"I have to prop the door open. Stay put." Once that was done, I went back to the Buick and unlocked the back door. Unhooking the seat belt around the basket, I involuntarily grunted as I hoisted the basket. It didn't help that the puppies were trying to escape.

Lugging the crate inside, I set it down on my slate floors. Whew! That was rough. Hearing a thump, I looked up to see Baby thudding his powerful tail against the glass wall, showing his typical delight that I was home.

"Give me a minute, Baby. I've got my hands full here." Fortunately, I hadn't yet stowed away Emmeline's playpen. I dragged it to the middle of the great room and lowered the laundry basket full of squirming puppies into it.

The last of my energy now gone, I sat on my mid-century blue and green couch, resting.

Baby, obviously miffed that I hadn't let him inside, thumped his tail harder against the glass wall in protest. Whining accompanied the thumping.

"Okay, Baby. I get the message!" I yelled.

Satisfied the little varmints were as secure as they could be, I strode over to open the patio door. Luckily, I had stepped aside because Baby zoomed past me to shove his snout into the playpen mesh. The excited puppies spilled out of the basket and rushed over, bringing themselves face-to-face with my agitated, two-hundred pound English Mastiff.

Fearing some calamity, I rushed over to grab Baby's collar to pull him away. Resisting my tugging, Baby emitted a high-pitched squeaking sound I had never heard before. He sniffed through the mesh and looked over the top of the playpen.

Baby was sweet with all the animals on the farm, but he was very territorial inside the Butterfly. I expected growling, but Baby appeared utterly delighted with the yipping little canines. He wagged his tail so energetically I was afraid he might topple over.

"Baby, who's a good boy? Who's a good boy? Do you see these critters as something to protect like your Kitty Kaboodle?" I cooed in my baby voice.

Baby's response was to turn his head around and look up at me, and, as strange as it sounds, I could swear he was smiling.

# 30

I got a call around ten at night, which woke the puppies. They desperately needed to potty, but I couldn't deal with them at the moment.

"Mrs. Reynolds, this is Eli Bradley. I was wondering if you talked to Hunter Wickliffe today. You mentioned you might stop by his house on your return from Louisville."

"No, I haven't," I answered in a sharp tone, still woozy from having awakened from a deep slumber.

"Why not?"

"Because life happened, Mr. Bradley. It wasn't opportune for me to speak with Hunter today."

"Do you plan to speak with him soon?"

"I don't know, Mr. Bradley. I've got my hands full."

"What could be more important than speaking with Mr. Wickliffe?"

"Puppies!" I retorted before slamming the receiver down on the landline cradle.

The puppies struggled to climb out of the laundry

basket, which I had placed in Emmeline's playpen. Lifting the basket, I carried it outside and let the puppies scurry about the backyard doing their business.

Baby followed, sniffing, and scooting the puppies with his nose. They responded by pulling on his ears with their sharp teeth and looking for milk-swollen teats. The mastiff was most confused by this behavior, but I didn't blame the puppies for being baffled. It had been a rough day for the little scoundrels.

After putting wet food in the makeshift paper bowls, I held onto Baby's collar as the dogs rushed to eat. "No, Baby, the food is not for you. I'll give you a treat later. Be patient."

The Kitty Kaboodle showed up when they heard the whimpers of the puppies and Baby's low-throated woofs. Two cats attempted to eat from the puppies' bowls, but the puppies' rambunctious nature caused all the cats to skedaddle into the Butterfly.

Baby jerked away from me, following the cats while the puppies followed Baby, nipping at his back legs.

After collecting the babies, I returned them to the laundry basket. It didn't take long for the cats to jump into the playpen, sniffing, licking, and finally tipping the basket over.

The puppies, delighted with their newfound friends, played too rough, so the cats climbed out.

The phone rang again. "HELLO!" I answered roughly.

"Did you say puppies?" It was Eli Bradley.

"Yes, and I've got my hands full. Right now I am entertaining Baby, his cats, and four puppies full of zip and zazz. Your call woke them up."

"Do you need any help?"

I looked at the receiver in confusion. "How can you help me?"

"I can come over."

"Good night, Mr. Bradley. Don't call me anymore. *I'll call you.*"

That was my first night with the puppies. It was a doozy. They finally fell asleep but woke me up at three, needing to go out. They weren't potty trained, so I made it my mission to let them out. Fortunately, they watched Baby tinkle and followed suit, but they took forever.

This was as bad as babysitting Emmeline. At least there were no dirty diapers to contend with. Utterly exhausted, I fell asleep on the couch with the lights on.

Of course, the cats woke me up at dawn.

Ugh. Sometimes I despise animals! They are so needy!

# 31

Waking up the next morning, I fed the menagerie and changed out of my filthy clothes from the night before. The cats retired to the barn after being fed, and an exhausted Baby plopped down by the playpen where I deposited the puppies again, who had kept us up most of the night. He quickly sank into a much-needed nap, and his steady breathing and closed eyes lulled the puppies into sleeping again, which meant I could take a catnap myself. As I drifted off, the Sandman sprinkled fairy dust on my eyes, and I fell happily into a dream of a man with lips like clover and lonesome like me.

Suddenly, sharp yips coming from the living room abruptly ended my date with Mr. Sandman's mystery man. I couldn't even remember my dreamboat's face. Oh well, it was nice while it lasted. Now for those rascally dogs!

I rose and staggered into the great room where the puppies were doing their business on my slate floors, having chewed through the playpen's mesh. I retrieved some zip ties from my junk drawer and made quick work of the hole and returned the escape artists to their confinement.

The doorbell rang.

Who could that be as I wasn't expecting anyone? I needed to answer, although I loathed doing so, but it might be an owner of a boarded horse needing assistance, or someone reporting my animals loose on Tates Creek Rd. My animals have pushed through the fences before. It was always a nightmare rounding them up.

Since I never answer the door unless I see who it is, I switched to the security app on my phone, which was hooked up to my new door camera. Take my advice—never open your door unless you see who it is, but I digress. On my front portico, I spied Eli Bradley clutching a myriad of bags. He was wearing a white cotton polo shirt and jeans—not his usual dark suit. He looked—I don't know—somehow arresting.

"What do you want, Mr. Bradley?" I spoke over the door camera speaker.

Bradley held the bags up to the camera. "I come bearing gifts."

"I told you not to call me."

"You never said anything about visiting."

Exasperated, I huffed, "I will see Hunter when it is convenient for me. He's not going anywhere."

"I'm leaving for Louisville today and wanted to say goodbye. I thought I might peek in on the puppies as well. I have toys for them." He held up the bags again, making a pitiful face.

"How did you get in?"

"You gave me the gate code for my last visit."

I almost laughed. "Okay, give me a moment." Still dressed in my nightgown, I put on a pink quilted robe and pink fluffy house slippers. Baby and I padded to the front steel double door and opened it with me holding onto Baby's collar.

"Let Baby smell you, Mr. Bradley."

Bradley stood quietly as Baby looked up at me for a hand signal. My mastiff sniffed Bradley's hand and jeans when I gave approval.

"That's enough, Baby," I commanded, pulling the dog out of the doorway. "Come on in, Mr. Bradley."

The man entered the foyer and strode over to the playpen, where the puppies eagerly watched. Dropping the bags, he picked up one puppy, who struggled to get free from his grasp. Bradley gently put him back in the playpen. "He didn't want to be petted."

"Sorry, they are not socialized yet. They are timid, and it will take some time for them to acclimate."

"I can see that."

"Mr. Bradley, why are you here? I said I would talk to Hunter, and I will in good time. You really shouldn't have come."

Bradley swiveled toward me. "Would you be nicer to me if I said my great, great uncle was Ed Bradley?"

"You mean Ed Bradley, owner of Idle Hour Farm? Winner of the 1921, 1926, 1932, and 1933 Kentucky Derbies?"

"Yeah. I was named after him."

"Wait a minute. Your name is Eli."

"Yes, Edward Riley Elijah Bradley."

"Elijah was not part of Bradley's name."

"Let's not split hairs. Elijah comes from my mother's side of the family."

"Only Calumet Farm has more Thoroughbred winners than your ancestor. Are you a devotee of the racing game, Mr. Bradley?" I had to admit I was impressed.

"I'm something of a gambler like my great uncle, but I bet on people's freedom. And call me Eli, please. I think we can dispense with the formalities after receiving me in your nightie."

I instinctively clutched the top of my frayed robe around my throat. "Call me Josiah then."

"I've been meaning to ask what gives with the name."

"My grandmother. That's all you need to know."

Eli seemed contrite. "I wanted to say goodbye before I left for Louisville."

"Why are you?"

"Leaving? I have other clients who need my personal attention. I can only do so much remotely."

"I see."

Turning his attention back to the playpen, Eli asked, "What are you going to do with the puppies?"

"Give them to good homes after I train them."

"May I have one?"

"No."

Eli looked hurt.

It immediately came to mind that Eli Bradley might be lonely. I knew this feeling all too well and regretted my harsh answer.

"Let me explain, Eli. I've been reading about these dogs, and they would not be suitable for your lifestyle."

"What are they? They look like regular mutts."

"They are a breed the European settlers brought with them into Kentucky during the 1700s. They are Mountain Curs."

"Never head of the breed."

"Neither had I, but they are rare. Have you ever read the book *Old Yeller*?"

"No, but I've seen the movie."

"Many think the dog described in the book is a Mountain Cur because its behavior mirrored that of one. These dogs were bred to be herders, hunters, and guards. If they are not with a dominant human and outdoors, they become depressed and therefore aggressive." As an afterthought I asked, "How many hours do you work?"

"Anywhere from fifty to seventy, depending on my caseload."

"This type of dog is not a good fit for you. I will find suitable homes for the puppies, most probably on a farm. Perhaps you are a cat person." I watched Eli with anticipation, hoped he would accept my suggestion.

"Naw, can't stand cats."

Disappointed, I remarked, "Too bad. Cats can be very amusing."

"I still would like to give the puppies their toys. I also got them a nice bed."

"That is very sweet of you." I paused for a moment, wondering how I could repay the man's kindness. "The dogs need a bath. Would you like to help? I'll wash and you dry."

Eli grinned. "Sounds most agreeable to me. Let's do it. I have to admit they stink."

I laughed. "Yes, they do. I have a medicated soap to use, and your lending a hand will be most helpful."

Eli picked up a yelping, quivering puppy, and we moved into the kitchen where I ran warm water in the sink. The temperate water calmed the yellow puppy as I lathered him with the medicated soap. He leaned into my hands and only fussed when I cleaned his ears. Rinsing him off, I handed the fur ball to Eli, who dried him thoroughly. After wrapping the dog in a clean towel, Eli gave him a treat and put him back in the playpen before picking up a new one.

It took an hour to wash all four puppies. I was

sweating from the effort, but Eli seemed happy, wearing a sloppy grin on his face. He looked almost handsome. I mean he was a good-looking man, but when smiling, Eli glowed with vitality. It was very appealing.

I noticed my sloppy appearance and remembered I hadn't brushed my hair. There was nothing I could do about it now. I had to brave my frumpy facade.

"This is the most fun I've had in a long time," Eli stated.

"It was fun for me, too." I glanced at the kitchen clock. "It's almost lunchtime. I have leftover pot roast if you are interested."

"I could stand something to eat before I leave," Bradley replied eagerly.

"Give me a few moments to put on fresh clothes. While I'm changing, can you take the puppies outside to do their business? Take Baby with you. They will stay close as long as he is with them."

"Sure thing."

I hurried to my suite and washed my face, combed my hair—and OMG!—I hadn't brushed my teeth either. I threw on a summer shift, sandals, and oh yeah, even put on a bra.

As I emerged from the bedroom and glanced outside, I spied Eli laughing and allowing the puppies to chase him. He acted like a kid, delighting in his new-found buddies. It was a shame he couldn't have one of the puppies, but I had to do what was best for them.

A sudden thought occurred to me. Was he the mystery man in my Mr. Sandman dream?

I realized I would miss Eli Bradley somewhat.

Just a tad, mind you.

<h1 style="text-align:center">32</h1>

Before I braved an encounter with Hunter, I had my hair, pedicure, and manicure done plus purchased a new outfit—one that fit tight in the right places and made me look great. You know—the eat-your-heart-out revenge outfit.

I didn't tell Hunter I was coming since he'd have locked the gates, so I had to surprise him. He wouldn't see me coming—sort of like Crazy Horse against Custer.

Keeping Lady Elsmere's Buick since my van was having repairs, I left Baby with the puppies. They would be fine until I returned.

However, the closer I traveled to Wickliffe Manor, the more nervous I became. What would I say—"*Hey, Hunter, did you murder your wife?*" Hoping to weasel the truth out of him, I wanted a quick in and a quick out visit. He had hurt me and speaking with him would be painful. I would give Hunter twenty minutes of my time.

Pulling into the entrance of Wickliffe Manor, I shut off the Buick. Did I really want to do this? Did I really want to see Hunter? Would he be pleased to see me? I guessed I would find out.

I restarted the car, crossed my fingers, and drove until I found myself outside of Wickliffe Manor. The red brick mansion appeared as steadfast and sturdy as she had always appeared. Oh yes, the house was a she. As I parked, the front door was open, so I honked.

There was no point in climbing the steep portico steps if Hunter refused to see me, but he came out, slamming the screen door as I scrambled out of the car. Surprised at seeing me, Hunter stopped, drying his hands on a dishtowel. He appeared thinner, almost gaunt, and his lack of grooming was telling. In short, Hunter looked defeated and tired.

"Am I welcome or not?" I inquired, not flinching beneath his blatant stare.

"Of course, you are," he assured, waving me up the limestone stairs. "I'm surprised to see you, that's all."

"I'm coming around to the kitchen door where there are no steps."

"I'll meet you there." Hunter went inside, slamming the screen door again, while I moseyed around to the back kitchen door where all I had to do was walk up a gentle grassy knoll. My bad leg, you see.

He held open the kitchen door. We both stood awkwardly in the doorway until I asked, "Are you going to let me through?"

He moved aside quickly and pulled out a kitchen chair. "Sorry, but I'm surprised to see you. It has thrown me."

"You've already said that," I scoffed, sitting down.

Hunter ran his fingers through his hair. "I guess I did. Where's Baby?"

"I left him at home. He's watching over the four puppies I rescued. He's a good babysitter."

"Puppies? How did you get puppies?"

"I didn't come to talk about that, Hunter. I'm here for a *Come to Jesus Moment.*"

"Josiah, don't. Please don't hammer me."

Seeing Hunter's expression, I decided to soften my approach to the talk we needed. "I'll give you one dog—maybe two. You need a dog on this farm. These are Mountain Curs—working dogs. Perfect for you."

Pulling a chair beside me, Hunter sat, pointing out, "Better give the puppy to someone else, Jo. I may not be around to take care of it."

"The trial is in four months, I hear."

"Do we have to talk about me? I want to hear what you've been doing."

"Yes, we do have to talk about you. That's why I'm here. Why are you sabotaging your defense?"

"Oh, I see. Did Bradley send you?"

"I would have come on my own, eventually. I don't understand why you confessed to a crime we both know you didn't commit."

Agitated, Hunter shot up from his chair. "How do you know I didn't kill Kathy?"

"Don't raise your voice at me and quit pacing. It's annoying."

"I don't want to talk about her," Hunter argued, clasping his fists together.

Why should I beg this man to tell me the truth? Hunter and I had shared confidences, danger, and even a bed. We had loved each other. Now all I saw was a stranger. Angry and frustrated at being put in the position of Hunter's confessor, I rose from my chair and slapped Hunter's face—hard. "Stop with the dramatics. You've caused me a great deal of heartache, and I deserve to know why. I was a genuine friend to you. I didn't merit being thrust aside like an old shoe."

Hunter bowed his head. "No, you didn't deserve it. I regret treating you the way I did. Always will!"

"Then tell me what happened with Kathy? Why did you marry her?"

"I feel so ashamed when I think of what I've done. You must hate me."

"Oh, I do, Hunter. I hate you, but I'll forgive you in due course—maybe a hundred years from now. My feelings are not at stake at the moment. It's getting you declared innocent or having the charges dropped. It's not only your life, but Franklin's, Emmeline's, Matt's, Palley's, and even mine when it comes down to it because we are so closely associated with you. The stench of this murder is rubbing off on all of us."

Hunter held out his hands as if begging. "I'm so sorry I've brought the repercussions of this incident upon you."

"*Incident!?* We're talking murder here. Do you really want to rot in jail?"

Hunter shook his head, looking away. His expression was one of abject misery.

"Explain what happened, Hunter. Share this burden with me."

"You know if I go to prison I will be in solitary confinement. They can't put me in the general population since I put so many of the inmates in there with my testimony. Jo, I don't know whether I could bear solitary confinement."

For a moment, my heart melted. "Let's sit down and hash this out. Just talk, Hunter. We can figure a way out of this. Come on. Sit down," I said, pulling at his shirtsleeve.

"Can't, Josiah. I really can't. I've tried, but there is no solution. No easy way out of this."

"Then you either killed Kathy or you are covering up for someone. Is it Palley? Did Palley kill his mother?"

Hunter refused to meet my gaze.

"If you won't talk, there's no use in browbeating you, but you're a fool, Hunter. A big, stupid fool."

"Don't scold me, Jo. I could use a friend. I need a friend."

"And you expect me to be such a friend? No dice. Why should I bear your lies, deceit, and narcissism? I think you really killed Kathy. I really do. All the evidence points to it."

Hunter seemed shocked. "Josiah!"

"I am not wasting sympathy on you, Hunter Wickliffe, if you won't help yourself. Why should I comfort you? I'm tired of being used by weak men. First my husband and now you. You can go to the blazes!" I stormed out of the kitchen door and made way for the Buick.

Was I truly angry? Yes and no, but I wanted to shake Hunter out of it, forcing him to take action to save himself instead of avoiding the topic. When he didn't follow, I wondered if I had pushed too hard. Maybe direct confrontation was the wrong approach?

This was a man living in isolation. Everything Hunter had worked for was in jeopardy. His career was over, and even if acquitted, Hunter would have to sell his ancestral home to pay Eli Bradley. Lawyers were not cheap. I would know.

I had spoken some awful truths. Here's another truth—I didn't feel better after having said them. In fact, I felt worse.

How could Hunter and I betray each other so when there had been such love between us?

One last truth—I was right about Hunter being a fool, but the biggest fool of all was me.

# 33

A tear ran down my cheek as I approached the car. Wiping it away, I dreaded calling Eli Bradley and telling him I had failed. Seeing Hunter was a mistaken strategy for Eli, and an emotional trap for me. Lordy, I'm such an idiot.

The screen door slammed again as I opened the car door. Hunter stood on the red-brick portico with hands in his jean pockets. Seeing I was determined to leave, Hunter ran down the steps, preventing my closing the car door.

"Josiah, don't go. Please come back inside. I know you are trying to help."

"Are you going to tell the truth or waste my time deflecting?"

"I'll answer anything you ask."

I must have given Hunter a disbelieving glance because he put a hand on my shoulder. "I swear."

A bolt of electricity ran up my spine at his touch. See what I mean about being stupid? "Swear on the

Bible that you'll tell the truth."

Hunter grinned. "Still a Southern Baptist girl at heart, eh, Josiah?"

I am not a churchgoing woman. I don't like church—never have—but I believe in the principles laid down by the Prince of Peace. So yes, I was going to make Hunter swear on the Bible after he helped me onto the portico.

He gathered his Bible, some iced-tea laced with bourbon, and sat down in a rocking chair beside me.

After he swore on the good book, we sat for a spell listening to the birds singing in the colossal oak and osage trees planted by his ancestors about Wickliffe Manor.

"Why did you marry Kathy?" I finally asked.

Hunter took a deep breath. "Kathy and I go way back. She was my first love. I wanted to marry Kathy, but she was impulsive and never thought about the consequences. When a man is young and inexperienced, this type of feminine energy seems attractive. I mistook Kathy's bubbliness and spontaneity for a person who loved living life on her terms and was not restrained by society's expectations. Kathy was exciting to be around. I loved being with her."

"And when she married Dwight Haskell?"

"I was devastated, of course. It wasn't until my senior when taking psych classes I realized Kathy might be ill. At the time, we called it Manic Depressive Disorder.

Because of her mental health issues, Kathy was impulsive, promiscuous, and reckless—not the impetuous but innocent beauty I thought her to be when we were in high school. I came to believe I had dodged a bullet. When I heard she had divorced Dwight, I felt sad for Kathy, but relieved it wasn't me."

"Yet you met her when both of you were in town. You both kept in touch over the years."

"Yeah, I slept with Kathy. She was beautiful, and I still felt a powerful connection with her. As long as our visits home were short, I didn't worry about becoming entangled with her. We spent a few sweet hours together now and then before returning to our lives."

"So you used her?"

Hunter snapped back. "We used each other. We were consenting adults, and I never slept with her while I was married."

"So you say."

"So I say, Josiah," he repeated heatedly.

"Did Kathy say she regretted not waiting for you?"

"No, she was truly in love with Dwight. I think she was remorseful the marriage didn't work. When we were together, we never talked about our current lives. Our conversations were about the past and our parents. It was very superficial."

"What happened when Palley was born?"

"I was living in Europe. Franklin told me Kathy had a baby, but I never assumed the child was mine. It could have been, but Kathy never contacted me, so I thought he was someone else's child. Kathy was always short of money. I knew if she thought the baby was mine, she would have asked for child support."

"Let's cut to the quick. Why did you marry Kathy?"

"What I say might hurt you, Jo."

"I'm a big girl. I can take it." I replied with confidence but braced myself for what I was about to learn.

"I loved you, but we didn't have a future. There was no going forward."

"I don't understand," I said, dumbstruck by Hunter's words. "I thought we were solid."

"I thought so too until Kathy came to me and said Palley was my son. She said the only way she would tell Palley is if I marry her."

"And that seemed okay with you?"

"I spent months debating my options. I believed her, and I had always wanted a child."

"This makes little sense. Palley was old enough to choose to see you on his own. He didn't need Kathy's permission."

"Those two were tight, and I knew if Kathy wanted, she would poison Palley against me."

"Did you love Kathy?"

"I loved the young Kathy—the girl I used to know. I didn't love or even like who Kathy had become, but it was a package deal—I take Kathy or nothing at all."

"Did you know Kathy had been arrested for petty

thievery, shoplifting, and then jailed for blackmail?"

"Not when I married her. I learned later. We had a fight, and she bragged about her past, laughing at what a fool I was."

I secretly thought the same thing as well, but kept those thoughts to myself. "When did you have this argument?"

"Several months before she passed."

"That's why you got the DNA paternity test done?"

"Yes. I took a glass Palley had used to a local lab and had his DNA wiped from it."

"Did Palley believe you were his father?"

"He thought Dwight Haskell was. I don't think he knew anything about me as a possible father."

"You and Dwight went to school together. You didn't see the resemblance?"

"I didn't want to see it. Besides, I haven't seen the man in years."

"Was Palley aware of Kathy's manipulation?"

"I think he was aware his mother had problems, but they were devoted to each other. For all of Kathy's idiosyncrasies, she was a good mother. I have to give her that."

I was in turmoil and needed time to process what Hunter had revealed, but I needed to get this interview over. It was killing me.

Taking a deep breath, I asked, "I have one last question. Did you murder Kathy?"

# 34

Hunter sought my gaze and held it. "I did not harm Kathy."

"Do you know who did?"

"I have my suspicions, but I'd rather not say."

"Tell me what happened that night."

"I heard a noise around two—two-thirty—something like that. It woke me up. I went to check on Kathy, but her bed had not been slept in, and Palley was nowhere to be found. A car fled up the driveway fast."

"Could you make it out?"

"I didn't get a good look, but it had throat."

"What does that mean?"

"It's a car term meaning loud like a muscle car."

"Okay, now what?"

"I guess I was still half-asleep, when I checked the house, Kathy's car, and last, the stable. I found her body in a terrible state, covered in congealed blood. The stable was a mess, as though there had been a fierce struggle. She was dead, with her eyes open and staring into nothingness."

"Then you framed yourself, wiping off the murder weapon and putting your fingerprints on it. You dragged Kathy's body into a stall and covered her in straw. All because you suspected Palley had killed his mother."

"No! No! The autopsy report said Kathy died around eleven that night. Palley wasn't even home that evening. He couldn't have done it."

I insisted, "He has an old beater, which is loud. That's the car you heard. You've suspected Palley from the start."

"If Palley killed Kathy, then why did he hang around for three hours before leaving?"

"Shock. Disbelief. Maybe he was high and needed to come down before he left?"

"I'm telling you—Palley could not have killed his mother. I don't want to discuss this further. You will not see reason."

"Me?" I had to keep my wits about me and suppress my anger. "Why hide Kathy under straw? Why leave her in the stable?"

"I thought Palley was with a girl and wouldn't be home. An owner of an Arabian horse was coming early in the morning to take her to another farm for breed-ing. I thought he would find Kathy and notify the police."

"But Palley came back early to care for the horses in the morning?"

"Yeah, I never thought he would come back until after Kathy was found."

"Everything you have said tells me you think Palley is responsible."

"I think it possible Palley found his mother around two and fled in horror."

"Oh, Hunter! This is an impossible theory. You're going down a rabbit hole. You've told lie after lie about who, what, and when, you've admitted to destroying evidence, and confessed to this crime. You even lie about your lies."

"Josiah, I know you are on the hunt. Don't dig up something that will hurt Palley."

"Hunter, did it ever occur to you that Palley may have inherited his mother's psychopathy? He may not be worth saving." I abruptly got up from my chair and made for the portico steps, hoping my movements weren't too jerky. My bad leg was acting up.

"Where are you going?"

"Far, far away from you. I'm so disgusted, I can't stand the sight of you."

"Josiah, please don't pull Palley into this. JOSIAH! JOSIAH!"

I didn't look back, didn't say goodbye, didn't promise.

My heart was aching.

What had Hunter meant when he said he realized we had no future together?

I wanted to get away from Wickliffe Manor before I broke down.

I needed a good cry and to get stinking drunk. There was a bottle of bourbon waiting for me at home. I was going to need it.

# 35

I took to the bed with quarts of Rocky Road ice cream, packages of Twinkies, baloney sandwiches, bags of chips, restocking my sugar buzz around the clock for several days. I was wallowing in self-pity and loving it.

Watching Rita Hayworth in *Gilda*, my favorite movie, I hissed and booed at the TV. A lover betrayals his great love, leaving her almost broken in spirit. He comes to his senses at the end and begs for forgiveness. Gilda takes the weasel back—what a fool. He'll just screw her over in the future. I threw my house slipper at the TV screen in protest.

I flipped on *The Letter* with Bette Davis, which was more to my liking. This movie starts with the heroine shooting her lover four or five times with a revolver— BANG—off the porch, BANG BANG—down the steps, and BANG—into the steaming tropical garden. That's what I wanted to see—romantic justice. Seeing Bette plug her boyfriend with lead filled me with glee. The thought of doing the same to Hunter made me happy—if it was only a fleeting notion.

My phone on the nightstand kept vibrating. I glimpsed at it. It was Eli Bradley whom I had been ducking for two days. Maybe it was time I answered his calls, so he would stop bugging me.

"Hello, Eli."

"Why haven't you answered my calls?"

I was not in the mood to kowtow at the moment. "I've not been feeling well." This was true as I was feeling queasy from all the sugar I had ingested.

"I'm so sorry to hear this."

I interrupted, "You want to know if I've spoken with Hunter?"

"Yes."

"The gist of our conversation was that he didn't kill Kathy, but he messed with the evidence because he feels Palley had something to do with her death, although he'll lie to your face in the next sentence and say Palley didn't. Oh, yeah, I'm not supposed to tell you this."

"Huh?"

"Everything Hunter has done was to protect Palley. The story he gives is one big convoluted pile of manure. You would need a shovel to sift through the half-truths and straight-out lies to get to the facts. Whatever you do, don't put Hunter on the stand. He'll lie to protect Palley."

"Are you saying Palley killed his own mother?"

"I'm saying Hunter thinks Palley is connected somehow. I really don't know if Palley did it or not, but Hunter will throw himself on the pyre to save that boy."

"I'll arrange to interview Palley. I haven't been able to get in touch so far."

"And you won't. I'll do it. I need to get out of bed anyway," I said, watching Baby doing zoomies in the backyard for the puppies' amusement.

"You don't need to, Josiah. I've asked enough of you."

"I'm not doing it for you or Hunter. I'm thinking of Franklin and Matt."

"Will you answer my calls now that you are feeling better?"

"Maybe." I turned off my phone without another word. Yes, I was rude, but I didn't care. If Eli knew what mental state I was in, he should be grateful that I was somewhat civil.

I swung my legs over the bed to the floor and was instantly nauseous. That was the bourbon talking. I've had hangovers before, but this one was a doozy. It was time to get over my grief as no man was worth this misery.

*Get off your fanny, Josiah*, I thought to myself. *Hunt down a murderer.*

And so I would.

# 36

Since I knew Palley loved old cars, I drove the Buick to where he worked. It was another sneak attack on my part. I was relying on the 1958 Buick Century to draw the boy out. I pulled into the garage and asked for an oil change. Knowing the car would cause a stir among the employees, I waited for news of it to make the rounds. Sure enough, Palley rushed out of the office to view the vintage red car with its white-walled tires.

"Oh, hello, Palley. I didn't know you worked here."

Startled, Palley peeked in the driver's window. "Mrs. Reynolds. This is a surprise. Is this beauty yours?"

"Heavens, no. I couldn't afford something like this. It's Lady Elsmere's. My van is being repaired."

"She sure is sweet," Palley said, eyeing every detail of the car with admiration.

"If you have a break coming up soon, I'll let you drive her."

"Really? Oh, gosh, yes. I have a lunch break coming up in twenty minutes."

"When the oil change is finished, I'll wait in the parking lot."

"You sure?"

"I've got nothing but time today."

Palley grinned and hurried back to work as his boss yelled his name. When finished with the oil change, I waited in the parking lot. The twenty-minute wait turned into thirty minutes, but I was patient. When Palley appeared, I scooted over the black leather bench seat to the passenger's side. Delighted to drive the Buick, he got in and felt the manual steering wheel, the chrome accenting the wooden dashboard, and the leather interior before turning the car on. "This baby is so dope. I love everything about it," he proclaimed, carefully driving onto the major thoroughfare.

I had to admit Palley was a handsome boy and seemed good-natured, but was he really? Sociopaths can be very charismatic. I needed to have a serious talk with him, but wanted to do it in a public place that possessed cameras. I suggested, "Palley, I could do with a hamburger myself. Why don't we head to the Sonic a few blocks away and get something to eat?"

"That would be cool. Sitting in a hot-looking car and ordering curbside. Now all we need are servers on roller skates to bring our food out."

"Palley, I think you were born in the wrong century," I chuckled.

"I love everything about the fifties and sixties.

When I make it big, I'm gonna build a house like the Butterfly." At the mention of the Butterfly, Palley's face fell when turning into the burger place. "You know this is the best I've felt since Mom died. Cars are my safe places. Driving this old Buick is a real treat for me."

"Glad I ran into you. You said at the visitation you wished to speak with me."

"I wanted to ask you—" Palley faltered.

"I will answer anything you ask of me, Palley," I encouraged in a soft voice.

"You were Hunter's girlfriend before he married Mom."

"Yes."

"Did Hunter leave you for Mom?"

"Yes, he did."

"Did Hunter tell you why?"

"Perhaps he loved your mother."

Palley fixed a worried gaze at me. "I don't think so. He was respectful to Mom, but his real bond was with me. I never understood why they married. They slept in separate rooms, and Hunter was distant. I didn't enjoy living at Wickliffe Manor. The house was too old and creepy."

"Old houses creak and groan."

"I'm living at my grandparents' home. I guess it is mine now. It's small but feels nice. Sort of a clean feeling when you walk in the front door. I always felt there were ghosts at Wickliffe Manor." Palley shivered.

"Have you spoken with Hunter since you . . . since your mother was found?"

"Not since the police arrested him."

"You really want to ask me if I think Hunter killed your mother."

Palley chirped hopefully, "Yes, I know about your reputation. Do you think Hunter killed my mother?"

"Honestly—no."

"Then why did he confess?"

"Why don't you tell me what happened that day?"

"Hunter and I repaired fences early, and Mom made lunch. During lunch, Mom said she wanted to go to a movie later that evening, but Hunter and I turned her down. Hunter needed to finish a report on a case, and I told her I had a date. This made her angry." Palley paused. "I need you to know my mom did everything possible for me, but she had problems."

"How so?"

"She would push boundaries. If she needed something, Mom would just take it. If I needed new sneakers to play basketball and she didn't have the money, she would steal them. She got caught shoplifting several times because of me. Went to jail for it. And if she didn't take her medication, her emotions became over the top. You know what I mean? I can't find the correct words to say what I mean."

"Was Kathy bipolar? Mood swings? Raw emotions? Bursts of anger? Spending sprees? Extreme energy on the other side of the coin?"

Palley's eyes widened. "Yes, exactly. That's what she said she was—bipolar, and she couldn't help her outbursts. Told me to ignore her anger."

"Tell me what happened during lunch."

"When Hunter said no, she got angry, but when I told her I had a date, she exploded. She screamed I was an ungrateful brat and worse. Even I don't use some words she called me. Hunter grabbed Mom and pushed her out into the backyard and locked the kitchen door on her. Told Mom through the door to calm down."

"Oh dear. That was the wrong thing to say. Never tell a woman to calm down."

"She threw rocks at the house, Mrs. Reynolds. Threw rocks! Who does that?"

"A woman who needs help, Palley. That was the disease talking. Not the woman who sacrificed her freedom so you could have new shoes. What happened next?"

"Hunter told me to pack a small bag and leave for the evening. Not to come back before morning. He gave me money for a hotel room."

That tidbit piqued my interest. "Did you spend other nights in a hotel room?"

"Yeah. Hunter would send me away when she got like this. I would go to the lodge at the state park. It was close and quiet. I could think there. When I returned the next day, Mom acted as though nothing had happened. I think Hunter gave her a pill or something."

"Let's go back to the fight that day. How did you respond?"

"I am ashamed of how I reacted. I told her that I hated her and wished she was dead. I threatened her."

"Did you mean it?"

"I did at the time. Mom would wear anyone down. I hated her disease. I couldn't take it anymore and wanted to be far away from her."

"Did you go on your date?"

"We went out for a couple of hours, but I wasn't in the mood. We played putt-putt golf, got something to eat, and then I took my friend home."

"Did you tell her about the argument?"

"No. Never. I didn't want people to know about Mom."

"Did you return to Wickliffe Manor the same day?"

"No, I got a room at the lodge."

"Hunter said he heard your car around two in the morning."

Palley looked surprised. "It wasn't me. I went to bed and only came back around six to check on the horses."

"Hunter said the car had throat. Throat means a car that rumbles—like your car."

Protesting loudly, Palley pleaded, "It wasn't me, I tell ya!"

"You asked me if I think Hunter killed your mother. No, I don't, but Hunter thinks you did. That's why he's taking the rap for her murder!"

# 37

Neither Palley nor I could choke down our burgers and shakes. Palley was upset, but relieved as pieces of the puzzle fell into place for him. We talked on the way back to his workplace, and he gave me vital pieces of information concerning his mother. After talking with him, I'm sure the police had confirmed Palley's whereabouts on the night of the murder, leaving Palley in the clear.

I also realized Walter Neff knew Palley was the person responsible for the hotel receipts when he threw out the clue about the lodge. I certainly fell for Walter's con and lost five-hundred dollars on a red herring. I would deal with Walter later.

Here's another thing I realized—Hunter lied to me again. Not one word about the argument that day. The only clue left was the car Hunter heard—the one with throat. If it wasn't Palley's car, whose then?

Since I was close by, I slowly drove past Palley's house in an established lower-middle-class neighborhood after Palley had given me the address. It was a sweet little wooden-frame bungalow with a well-tended front yard shaded by large ginkgo trees, probably built after WWII for veterans coming home.

And there sitting in the driveway was a rusty 1974 Plymouth Barracuda—a muscle car which had throat.

Well, well, wasn't that special?

# 38

Baby and I were hawking my honey at the farmers' market when Dwight Haskell marched up to my booth, mad as a wet hen.

Haskell was dressed in ragged jeans and a thin green button-up cotton shirt. He must have been working on a car as he had grease on his hands. "I want to talk to you," he snarled.

I admit Dwight's sudden appearance threw me off balance. "I can talk with you later, but this is my place of work."

He jabbed a finger at me. "You stay away from Palley. He wants nothing to do with you. You're trying to pin something on him to help your boyfriend."

"If you're referring to Hunter Wickliffe, he is not my boyfriend. It was Palley who wished to speak with me."

Alarmed at the angry tone of Dwight's voice, Baby pressed into my legs and growled with his fur standing up on his hackles. "Mr. Haskell, you are upsetting my dog. Please lower your voice."

"Why don't you bother John Sturgeon? I hear he's still in town. He had a fat insurance policy on Kathy."

"Does he have a car that is loud?"

"What?"

"Hunter said he heard a loud car the night of Kathy's murder. The only two people connected to this case with loud cars are Palley and you. Were you at Wickliffe Manor the night of Kathy's death?"

"Hunter Wickliffe is a bald-faced liar."

"Yes, he lied when he confessed to killing Kathy. You didn't answer my question—were you at Wickliffe Manor the night of Kathy's death?"

Haskell moved closer and jammed his finger close to my nose. "You stay away from me and Palley, you hear or else."

"Or else what? Sounds like a threat."

"It is. Quit sticking your nose in our business. Palley has enough to deal with." Haskell looked down as Baby growled at him. "And keep your mangy mutt on a tight leash."

"Is there a problem here?"

Haskell and I turned to see my old pal, Detective Kelly, holding a hot chocolate and a bag filled with glazed donuts.

"No, Detective." I emphasized the word *detective* when speaking. "Mr. Haskell was leaving."

Haskell scowled at us both before storming off.

"What was that about?" Kelly asked.

"He was angry I had talked to his son."

"So?"

"His son is Palley—Kathy Wickliffe's boy."

Kelly raised his eyebrows. "Are you snooping around, Jo? You know Detective Drake wouldn't like it. He's the lead man on Kathy Wickliffe's case."

My response to being confronted was always the same: I went on the attack. "Tell me why the DA also has Walter Neff investigating? Isn't he stepping on your toes? I know you guys are very territorial."

Let me give you some background on Kelly. He dated my daughter in high school. After their breakup, Kelly went into law enforcement, and as a beat cop, he would always bring hot chocolate and donuts to my booth. I was very fond of Kelly and wished he and my daughter had married, but it was not to be.

"He follows up on minor details when we don't have time. He's second string. How did you know Walter was working on this case?"

"Lady Elsmere," I lied.

Kelly narrowed his eyes. "Are you sure?"

"Tell me this. Was Kathy still married to John Sturgeon? He said he and Kathy had never divorced."

"When did Sturgeon tell you this?"

"At Kathy's funeral, but I thought he was lying." I could tell Kelly disapproved of my going to Kathy's funeral. "Well, is it true?"

"If he discussed this with you, then I can confirm we found no record of John Sturgeon and Kathy Wickliffe divorcing, which gives Hunter motive."

"Oh, stop it. We both know the DA is showboating. That wouldn't give Hunter a motive. It would give him an easy way out of the marriage. If anything, it gives Sturgeon motive—anger at Kathy running out on him and a fat insurance policy."

"How did you know about the policy?" Kelly asked, both awed and exasperated at my knowledge of the case.

"The man you ran off—Dwight Haskell—told me."

"Still Hunter confessed."

"He recanted."

"I can't discuss this with you, Josiah. Enjoy your drink and donuts."

He started to walk away.

I grabbed his arm. "Hey, wait a minute. Would you like honey in exchange for the donuts? I have two bottles of delicious clover honey left. I harvested it three weeks ago. Or would you like a carton of eggs? These are pretty eggs—mostly blue and green." I raised various breeds of chickens, which laid colored eggs. No joke.

"I'll take the honey, please," Kelly gushed, his face brightening up at the prospect of fresh honey.

I put the honey in a paper bag and handed it to Kelly.

"Stay out of trouble, Josiah," Kelly warned before departing.

"Sure thing, Detective." Watching Kelly make his way through the market crowd, I thought of how Kelly was such a decent man. I wished my daughter hadn't broken up with the man. I would have had grandchildren by now.

Baby nudged me for a donut. Reaching into the bag, I gave him one, which he inhaled.

"Don't you chew anymore?"

Baby nudged me for another donut.

"No, the last one is mine."

The market was winding down, and I used the free time thinking about what bits of information I had confirmed in the last two days. The police had ruled out Palley as a suspect, and Kathy had never divorced John Sturgeon, who had a large insurance policy on her.

Hmm, John Sturgeon just rose on my suspect list.

Maybe it was time I spoke with Kathy's best friend, Amanda Prescott.

# 39

I googled Amanda Prescott and wrote her address down on a scrap of paper. Then I called Agnes Bledsoe and asked her if she knew where Amanda worked. She didn't know, but thought Hunter might. Since I didn't wish to speak to Hunter, I called Eli and asked him.

"I'm in court right now. Let me call you back in five."

I hung up and waited while sipping tea on the patio watching the puppies play with Baby. A few of my free-range chickens waddled over to inspect the new creatures. Once realizing the puppies were not food, many drifted away, pecking on the ground while a curious few stayed at the fence watching the spectacle of brown fur streaking past.

My phone rang. It was Eli. "Why do you want Prescott's address?"

"I want to talk to her."

"I've already spoken with Miss Prescott. She's hesitant to talk."

"Let me try. I'm good with people."

"That you are. You sure were good with Palley. That was excellent intel you got from him. I haven't confronted Hunter yet, but I plan to do so soon."

"By the way, after I speak with Amanda Prescott, I plan to visit the State Fair, so I'll be in Louisville. I want to see if I've won any ribbons. I saw the rabbits, goats, and sheep will be there as well."

"Perfect. I'll join you. We can do the sights and match notes. Tell me what time."

"I don't know. It depends if I can get hold of Prescott. Say I call you around noon and see."

"Deal. I'll wait for your call." Eli hung up.

I don't know why, but I was pleased Eli wanted to visit the Kentucky State Fair with me.

Hunter never wanted to visit the fair.

Remembering made me angry, and as the afternoon wore on, the memory turned into a blister.

# 40

The next morning I walked into a charming insurance office in downtown Nicholasville and asked for Amanda Prescott. The sign outside said Prescott LLC, so Amanda Prescott must own the business.

A young, sprightly receptionist smiled until she spied Baby and blanched. "We don't allow dogs in the office. I'm so sorry."

"He is my support dog. I don't go anywhere without him," I said. It was a lie about Baby being a support dog, but I don't like leaving him in a car on hot days.

The receptionist pursed her lips. "May I tell Miss Prescott who's calling?"

"Tell her it is Josiah Reynolds about Kathy."

The receptionist's cheeks flushed as she gave an icy glare. "I've read about you in the papers, Mrs. Reynolds."

I was astonished the young woman recognized me. "Could you announce me, please?"

"Ah, yeah, sure." The young woman knocked on a

door and stuck her head in. A few seconds later, the receptionist swung the door open and beckoned me. Baby and I walked smugly past her into a comfortable office fitted with lots of potted plants, especially ferns.

Amanda Prescott rose to greet me. She was a stunning-looking brunette wearing a tailored navy suit with white piping. We shook hands, and she petted Baby. "I saw you at Kathy's funeral, Mrs. Reynolds."

"Yes, but we didn't get a chance to speak."

"Was there a reason to speak to each other?"

"I wanted to ask you about Kathy."

Prescott looked doubtful. "What was there to ask?"

"Specifically, I wanted to ask about John Sturgeon."

"He was there as well. Why come to me?"

"I want to get your opinion. Did you know him?"

"Are you working for the paper, Mrs. Reynolds?"

"Goodness, no. You know my reputation. I'm trying to discover the truth. Did you know John Sturgeon?"

Prescott looked convinced and tapped a pencil on her desk. "Not personally. Only what Kathy told me. He was a good provider, lousy in bed, and controlling. She wasn't happy in the marriage."

"I want to know if you knew of any insurance policy on Kathy."

Prescott pressed her lips together, deciding if she should tell me the truth. She glanced at Baby lying on the floor and smiled. "I have a Newfoundland at home.

I love big dogs."

"Miss Prescott?"

Kathy's friend looked up from Baby, saying, "Kathy, Hunter, Franklin, and I ran with a small circle of friends back in the old days. We spent most of our time at Wickliffe Manor riding horses, swimming in the river, listening to records, and cruising around town. It was an innocent time."

"I wasn't aware you knew Hunter."

"I knew the entire Wickliffe family."

"So you knew Agnes Bledsoe."

"I knew Agnes somewhat. She was older than us and an employee. I didn't have much to do with her."

"But you and Kathy kept in touch after high school?"

"Yes, that relationship took. I liked Kathy very much—when she was in her calm phase."

"What did you think of Kathy marrying Dwight?"

"The three of us were from the same economic background and from the same neighborhood. Kathy and I were both smart and thrown into advanced classes with Hunter. That's how we became part of his social circle. When Hunter left for college and Kathy took up with Dwight, I was shocked. Hunter was everything a girl wanted—looks, good background, smart, hard worker, and a bright future. For a girl like Kathy, who came from the poor part of town, Hunter was a catch. Dwight was a hard worker too, but his drinking kept him down. I was not enthused about their relationship, and of course, I was right when they divorced after a few years. I will say this for Dwight—he was handsome and charming when young. I could see the temptation because Kathy had no willpower when it came to men."

"You're the second person to say that about Dwight. Do you know anything about a life insurance policy John Sturgeon took out on Kathy?"

"I wrote it up."

"You did?"

"It was right before they got married when Kathy asked me to draw it up. They signed it in this office. John also had one taken out himself for 500k with Kathy as the beneficiary. It was Kathy's idea for the policies."

"Do you think John could have had something to do with Kathy's demise?"

Prescott seemed doubtful. "I don't know. He wasn't easy to live with, but the main friction was between John and Palley—not John and Kathy."

"I've learned there were police calls to their house in California. Did Kathy tell you?"

"Yeah, that was because of her. She would fly off the handle because of her illness. She was bipolar and didn't take her medication regularly. Palley would call the police when she got out of control."

"So, the calls weren't because of Sturgeon then?"

"Goodness, no. That man was besotted with Kathy and tried to help. Palley wanted to come back to Kentucky where his grandparents lived, but they died soon after the move to California where John had his practice."

"I see," I replied, subconsciously rubbing my arm where Sturgeon had left a bruise. I wasn't sure whether I believed Prescott about Sturgeon. After all, she was getting her information from Kathy, who might have been too embarrassed to tell the truth. "Will Sturgeon get his insurance money?"

"After someone is convicted for killing Kathy. It might take years before this matter is resolved, but Sturgeon hasn't even submitted a claim."

"He hasn't?"

"In fact, I asked him about it at the funeral, and he replied, 'Why does the money matter now?'"

"Is there anything else you would like to tell me before I take my leave, Miss Prescott?"

"I suspect you are acting on Hunter's behalf. Off the record, I don't think Hunter killed Kathy—not the man I *knew* in high school. I am surprised he married Kathy, but what do I know about human relationships? I've been single all my life. Been a bust at romance. It turned out every man I dated was a frog."

It was a shame Amanda Prescott was withering on the vine as she was a knockout. Maybe men were threatened by her beauty and success. Who knows? I'm a bust at romance myself.

I rose, as did Baby. "Thank you. I appreciate your time."

"Tell Hunter I'm rooting for him," Prescott said earnestly.

"I will. He will appreciate your good wishes."

Amanda Prescott walked me to the front door of her office building before giving Baby one last pet on the head. Too bad she couldn't have been more of a positive influence on Kathy, but then who could tame a whirlwind?

# 41

Around noon, Eli Bradley joined me at the food pavilion, where I was purchasing a corn dog for Baby and a hot dog for myself. He got a bratwurst and a large mug of beer.

"You've got foam on your upper lip," I mentioned.

He chuckled and wiped it off. "I haven't been to the State Fair since I was a boy. You come every year?"

I nodded. "Mostly for the honey competition, but I like to see the animals."

Before taking a huge bite of his bratwurst, Eli stated, "You like animals."

"Better than people."

"I hope you like me."

I didn't know how to respond, as it took me by surprise, so I inquired about Hunter.

Eli wiped some mustard from his face—just between you and me, the man was a messy eater. "It looks hopeless. Everything points to the man's guilt. We did another polygraph test, which indicated Hunter was not involved with Kathy's death. I compared the questions to the first polygraph test and rearranged the wording of the questions, but that's the only thing in Hunter's favor."

"What about Dwight Haskell and John Sturgeon?"

"The police checked their alibis for eleven o'clock, and they are solid. They even gave DNA, and theirs wasn't on Kathy's body."

"The woman was violently assaulted. There has to be some DNA on her."

Eli shrugged.

"What about the muck shovel?"

"DNA tests were done. It's Hunter's."

"Was the entire shovel tested? I bet it was just tested around Hunter's fingerprints on the handle."

"Hmm. That's a thought. I'll look at the report again and maybe order a new DNA test."

"Was Hunter's DNA found on her body?"

"No."

"You don't find that strange? The woman had been in an altercation, and no DNA was found on her clothes?"

"We think her face, arms, and hands were wiped clean."

"So Hunter wiped his DNA off her body but left fingerprints on the shovel? Come on, Eli! Even a rookie attorney could shred that bit of evidence."

"Other than that, Mrs. Lincoln, how did you like the play?"

"Exactly," I fumed. "Anything else?"

"I had my men take pictures at the visitation and funeral. The police did as well."

"So I noticed. It was a bit of an overkill, no pun intended."

Eli got out his phone and scrolled through it. "We have identified everyone but this man. Do you know who he is?"

I peered at the picture of a squat, balding middle-aged man wearing a green sports jacket. "Make the picture larger, please."

Eli handed me the phone, so I fiddled with it until I saw something I recognized. "I think he is a horse person. He's got a Keeneland Club pin on his lapel." I peered closer at the image. "It's a 1985 Keeneland pin. Kind of rare."

"Then he's associated with the Thoroughbred industry."

"Perhaps, or he could be a fan. Listen, send that picture to me. I'll show it to Lady Elsmere. She knows everyone."

Eli grinned. "Sure thing. Now that our business has concluded, can we enjoy ourselves? I want to see those bunny rabbits."

"I want to see if I have won any ribbons for my honey."

"You show the way, Josiah. This is within your purview." Eli gave the rest of his bratwurst to Baby, took a last swig of his beer, and helped me to my feet. We were off to the beekeepers' competition pavilion.

As we finally approached the display of honey submissions, I handed Baby's leash to Eli and rushed ahead to see how I had fared in the competition. The first thing I saw was a shiny ribbon affixed to my light honey. Drat! Third place. I had been robbed! I was a little buoyed by my clover entry—second-place ribbon! Yes, there was some justice in the world. I proceeded down the far end of the display case and was crushed to see my Wildflower fall honey had no ribbon at all. On second thought, there was no justice in the world. However, one of my honey frames had a ribbon—the coveted blue ribbon. I was a happy girl—three ribbons out of five submissions. Pretty darn good.

After perusing the rest of the honey exhibit, we visited the vegetable exhibit. I just had to see if the thousand-pound pumpkin won the weight contest. After discovering a larger pumpkin had won, we went to the livestock pavilion where we petted bunnies, various breeds of goats and sheep until we were asked to leave as the sight of Baby made the billy goats feisty. They wanted to fight my dog and were butting their cages, trying to get at him. Not wishing to cause a canine-goat war, we obliged and left.

Eli and I parted at the parking where I caught a tram to my car. Waving goodbye, I realized I was glad Eli had joined me.

It had been a happy three hours, and in those three hours, I hadn't thought of Hunter once.

# 42

Baby plodded into Lady Elsmere's kitchen first, with me following and carrying a laundry basket of leaping puppies, trying to see over the rim of the basket.

Bess was at the kitchen sink peeling apples. "What have you got there?"

"I've come bearing gifts."

"Don't you dare palm puppies off on us," Bess ordered, her arms akimbo.

I glanced at the knife she was carrying and put the basket on the table. "Pick one up, Bess. You know you want to."

"Get that dirty basket off my clean table, Josiah."

I scooped up a puppy and went over to Bess, caressing her brown cheek with the dog's fat, squirming body. Bess melted when the puppy licked her face with its wet little tongue.

"I hate you, Josiah. I really do," Bess pouted, now hugging the puppy.

"I'll be giving them away in a month. I need to train

them first. Shall I mark you down as taking one? How about two? They love company."

Bess returned the puppy to the basket, where the other three jumped on their hind legs, trying to get her attention. "Maybe, and only a maybe. Get out of here with those varmints. Their fur is getting everywhere and on my apples."

"Where is she?"

"If you mean Her Ladyship, she's having tea in the parlor with a few of her bridge cronies."

"Those old bags."

"Yes, those old bags."

"I'm going to crash it."

"Your funeral."

"Come on, Baby, let's misbehave." I picked up the puppies and proceeded to the parlor, where afternoon tea was officially served.

"Oh, hello. I didn't know you had company, Lady Elsmere," I said, bursting into the room. I laid the basket down on the floor, letting the puppies run wild. One immediately ran over to one old lady and jumped on her legs, demanding to be petted. He put a run in her stockings.

Lady Elsmere gave me a dirty look until one puppy whimpered at her feet. She picked the puppy off the floor only to cuddle it. Taking their cue from Lady Elsmere, the others ceased their complaints.

I sat next to an old harridan on the settee. When she

gave an alarmed look, I patted her lap and asked, "Howdya do?"

Now let me set you straight. I have nothing against old ladies. I'm going to be an old lady myself, but these three bridge-playing gals of Lady Elsmere were venomous gossips. They'd put a rattlesnake to shame.

Letting the puppy nibble her earlobe, Lady Elsmere asked regally, "Is there something you needed, Josiah?"

"Yeah, I do." I pulled my phone out and clicked on the picture of the strange man at Kathy's visitation. "Do you know who this is?" I asked, handing Lady Elsmere the phone.

Lady Elsmere put on her bejeweled reading glasses and studied the picture before handing the phone over to her friends. "It is Hamish Nathaniel Bamford III. Why do you want to know?"

One lady confirmed the man's identity before handing the phone to her friends, "Yes, that is Hamish."

I told the ladies, "His name is not familiar to me. What can you tell me about him?"

"He's originally from Great Britain but has lived here since a teenager. His father was in import-exports—a self-made man who dabbled in horse racing. After he passed, his son, Hamish also dabbled in racing, winning several stakes, but never making it to the big time. I heard he switched from Thoroughbred racing to trotting, where he had more success. I haven't seen the man in ages."

"Neither have I," admitted one harridan. The other two nodded in concurrence.

"I remember one thing about Hamish," recalled Lady Elsmere. "He had a fondness for seafood, especially shrimp. Why do you want to know?"

"Does he have anything to do with Hunter Wickliffe's case?" asked another lady, rescuing her purse from the jaws of a puppy happily gnawing.

I put the doggies in the basket while ignoring the flood of questions now thrown at me. "Thank you so much, ladies. Nice seeing ya'll again."

Fearing a myriad of questions, I rushed out of the parlor, fleeing for my life.

# 43

I gave the information to Eli twenty minutes later. He promised he would check into Hamish Nathaniel Bamford III, but cautioned I shouldn't hope this lead would pan out. Sometimes I thought Eli Bradley didn't want Hunter to be found innocent. He wasn't as optimistic about Hunter's chances as I was.

"You need to take this seriously, Eli. A little bird told me that Kathy was blackmailing this man for years and had recently approached him for more money. He turned her down, which might have made Kathy mad. Get this guy's DNA and have it tested against the muck shovel or anything else in the stable."

"Who told you this?"

"Agnes Bledsoe, who said she had lunch with the man recently."

"That's hearsay, and why would he confess to this Mrs. Bledsoe?"

"Because they are buddies and go way back in the horse business. He only admitted to Kathy blackmailing him—not that he murdered her, which is why you've got to get the DNA tests done. You need to place the man in the stable. Even have the horses tested. He would most probably handle their halters."

"I don't know, Josiah. This sounds like a long shot to me. It will cost Hunter a lot of money and may prove to be faulty info."

"Eli, are you going to fight for your client or not? If no, then step aside."

"Alright. Alright. Don't get your back up. My, you have a temper."

"Then do it, Eli." I slammed the phone down.

44

Days turned into weeks, then a month. Blistering August melted into mild September days. I heard nothing from Eli or Hunter. Neither had Franklin nor Matt contacted me. We were all wondering what was happening with Hunter's case—apparently nothing.

I was sorry I had been so brisk with Eli the last time I spoke with him. I wondered if he hadn't called because he was angry. Hunter's trial was only three months away, and I hadn't received any subpoena from the DA's office yet. They hadn't even asked to interview me. Neither had the police sought me out again. Not even Walter Neff contacted me.

The silence was deafening.

One evening my doorbell rang. I looked on my phone security app, and it was Eli Bradley, holding up a bottle of champagne tied with a bow.

Baby and I opened the door.

Eli pushed past me into the great room. "I've got news, Josiah. Get me some glasses first. Hurry! Hurry!"

"What is it, Eli?" I asked, rushing to get two champagne flutes out of the cabinet.

"Wait until I make a toast."

I put the glasses on my dining table while Eli popped the cork. After pouring the champagne, he handed me a glass. "Now I'm making a toast. To the stalwart Josiah Reynolds and her bad-ass attorney friend, Eli Bradley—Mr. Hunter Wickliffe is an exonerated man. The charges were dropped three hours ago, his ankle bracelet has been removed, and the announcement will be on the five o'clock news. Kiss me right here." Eli pointed to his cheek.

I gave him a quick peck.

We both took a drink of the champagne.

"Tell me what happened. I was getting worried."

"I took the information about Bamford and ran with it. I had the murder weapon retested, and you were right. The police only had it tested for DNA around Hunter's fingerprints. The lab found unidentified male DNA near the tip of the handle. Then I had to track down this Bamford guy and get his DNA without him knowing it. My guys rooted through the man's garbage and pulled out a toothbrush. The DNA was a match. I gave the evidence to the district attorney, and she had the police pull him in for questioning."

"Was Bamford evasive?" I asked.

"No, his answers were plausible, but they checked

his cell phone records, and it pinged near Wickliffe Manor on the night of Kathy's murder. My theory is Kathy kept pestering him for money and threatened to expose him."

"That's my take on it."

"This cast doubt on the DA's theory of the case, and she had Hunter hauled in for more questioning. This time he answered the questions truthfully, admitting he thought Palley had killed his mother and tried to cover it up. He will be charged with evidence tampering and making false statements to the police. I'm sorry to say, even though Hunter won't face a murder trial, his career as a forensic psychiatrist for the courts is over."

"What made the police believe Hunter?"

"Hamish Bamford must have gotten nervous after the police interview and tried to flee on a horse cargo plane bound for South America as a stowaway. What he didn't realize was the police had put a surveillance team on him. They arrested him at the airport on *suspicion of murder*. They have more loose-ends to tie up, but I think they've got the right man this time."

"Did Bamford have a loud car?"

"Funny you should say that. He needed a new muffler on his car. Bamford said he hit a pothole on the Wickliffe's gravel driveway and broke it."

"But why stay so long at the farm? Hunter said he heard a loud car around two-thirty."

"My take is that Bamford realized he dropped something during the struggle and went back for it."

"I'm so happy for Hunter."

"Ah, a pox on Hunter Wickliffe." Eli put down his glass and swept me into his arms, giving an ardent kiss. When he released me, Eli smiled a rakish grin. "I'll be phoning you, Josiah Louise Reynolds. You'd better answer."

Then he left me in a daze, standing with my mouth gaping open.

What just happened?

# 45

Six weeks later, I pulled in front of Wickliffe Manor and honked the horn on my repaired VW van.

Hunter opened the front door and stepped out onto the portico. "Josiah, why are you here?"

"Glad to see you too, Hunter."

"I always say the wrong thing."

"Yeah, you do. You staying or selling the farm?"

"Don't know yet. I sold five acres, which should cover my legal fees. I also cashed in a small insurance policy on Kathy. It will help until work comes along."

"That means you're staying. Good." I opened the door to my van, and two Mountain Cur dogs spilled out and, upon seeing Hunter, they ran up the steps to the portico.

"What is this?"

"Your new dogs, Hunter. They are the Mountain Cur puppies I found."

"They don't look like puppies anymore."

"No, they don't. I've trained them. They follow

commands, love to ride in cars, will herd your cattle, and guard the house. They are potty-trained and socialized—good with children and will guard Emmeline to their death. They are working dogs, Hunter, and must be active. Do you accept them?"

Hunter peered down at the two fawn-colored dogs sitting at his feet and staring up at him. "Yes, I accept. How much do you want for them?"

"A good home for the rest of their lives. Now, if for some reason, you can't keep them, give them back to me. Don't re-home them with someone else. Promise."

"I swear."

"Okay then. I hope the three of you will be very happy together." I climbed into my van.

"Wait a minute, Josiah." Hunter rushed from the portico and stood by the driver's window. The dogs followed.

"What?" I asked, turning the car key. The van came to life.

"Do you think we could talk sometime?"

"About?"

"Us."

"I don't know, Hunter. I'll have to see." I put the van in drive and drove away. Looking in the rearview mirror, I spied Hunter watching me leave and the dogs chasing after the van.

It was heartbreaking.

The End.

Josiah's phone won't stop ringing. Both Hunter Wickliffe and Eli Bradley are vying for her attention. At first it was flattering and fun, but now she doesn't have a moment's peace. Meanwhile, Josiah and her dog, Baby, take their daily walk to give treats to the horses and llamas before checking the mailbox. Baby is occupied with sniffing out the scents left overnight by the rabbits, foxes and coyotes, as Josiah leafs through the bills and junk mail. A small blue envelope at the bottom of the stack catches her attention. It is just inscribed with **JOSIAH** above her address in crude block letters. There is no return address. She quickly tears it open, and a single sheet of paper falls to reveal one word.

## DEATH!

## GET JOSIAH'S NEXT MYSTERY NOW!

# Other Books By Abigail Keam

## Josiah Reynolds Mysteries

# Mona Moon Mysteries

# Last Chance For Love Series

# About The Author

Hi, I'm Abigail Keam. I write the award-winning and international best-selling author of the *Josiah Reynolds Mystery Series* and the *1930s Mona Moon Mystery Series*. In addition, I write *The Princess Maura Tales* (Epic Fantasy), the *Last Chance For Love Series* (Sweet Romance), and the *Asa Short Stories*.

I am a professional beekeeper and have won awards for my honey from the Kentucky State Fair. I live in a metal house with my husband and various critters on a cliff overlooking the Kentucky River. I would love to hear from you, so please contact me. Until we meet again, dear friend, happy reading!

You can purchase books directly from my website: www.abigailkeam.com